Allie could only stare as [he closed] the distance betw[een them]

"What about you?" De[rek reached] out toward her a[s if to touch her,] then he fisted hi[s hand and put his] arm back to his side. [Any secrets] you'd like to share[?]

She swallowed in an [atte]mpt to work moisture back into her mouth. "Nothing quite as dark as arachnophobia."

"You sure?" His eyes were steady. Intense. "Because you know what they say about confession being good for the soul."

Except she didn't need confession. Not when she'd already taken care of her penance on her own.

"I'm positive."

"Everyone has secrets, Allison. And I'm guessing yours are more interesting than most." He leaned forward, and she slanted away. "Guess I have my work cut out for me," he murmured.

Fear, irrational and unsettling, filled her. "What work is that?"

One side of his mouth lifted. "Finding out what your secrets are."

Dear Reader,

I was seventeen when my best friend's mother gave me a Harlequin novel to read. I was immediately hooked, but between finishing school and figuring out what I wanted to do with my life, my reading time dwindled.

It wasn't until after I was married and became a young stay-at-home mother that I rediscovered Harlequin books. I became so addicted, I read while my son napped as well as when I cooked, ran the vacuum and worked out on the stairclimber!

No matter what type of story I was in the mood for—passionate, suspenseful, humorous or sexy—Harlequin had the book for me and, best of all, each one had a satisfying central love story and a happy ending.

It was during this time of rediscovery that I realized exactly what I wanted to do with my life. I wanted to be a romance author for Harlequin Books.

That dream came true on August 21, 2007, when I sold my first book to Harlequin Superromance. I have to say the reality of writing for this publisher is better than anything I'd ever imagined, and a large part of that is due to the guidance and patience of my wonderful editor, Victoria Curran, and Harlequin Superromance's senior editor, Wanda Ottewell.

This year Harlequin Books is celebrating sixty years of pure reading pleasure. Whether you've read these books for years or have recently discovered them, I hope you'll join me in wishing Harlequin a happy sixtieth birthday!

Thank you for reading *His Secret Agenda.* I hope you enjoy Allie and Dean's story! I love to hear from readers. Please visit my Web site, www.bethandrews.net, or write to me at P.O. Box 714, Bradford, PA 16701.

Beth Andrews

His Secret Agenda
Beth Andrews

HARLEQUIN®

TORONTO • NEW YORK • LONDON
AMSTERDAM • PARIS • SYDNEY • HAMBURG
STOCKHOLM • ATHENS • TOKYO • MILAN • MADRID
PRAGUE • WARSAW • BUDAPEST • AUCKLAND

Recycling programs
for this product may
not exist in your area.

ISBN-13: 978-0-373-71591-6

HIS SECRET AGENDA

www.eHarlequin.com

Printed in U.S.A.

ABOUT THE AUTHOR

Award-winning author Beth Andrews is living her dream—writing romance for Harlequin Books while looking after her real-life hero and their three children. A self-professed small-town girl, Beth still lives in the Pennsylvania town where she grew up. She has been honored by her kids as The Only Mom in Town Who Makes Her Children Do Chores and The Meanest Mom in the World—as if there's something wrong with counting down the remaining days of summer vacation until school starts again. For more information about Beth or her upcoming books, please visit her Web site at www.bethandrews.net.

Books by Beth Andrews

HARLEQUIN SUPERROMANCE
1496—NOT WITHOUT HER FAMILY
1556—A NOT-SO-PERFECT PAST

To Mom and Dad for always believing in me.
I love you.

CHAPTER ONE

DEAN GARRET HAD TWO WORDS to describe the town of Serenity Springs, New York.

Freaking cold.

And to think just last week he'd been complaining about the weather in downtown Manhattan. Guess mid-February wasn't the best time to head north into the Adirondack Mountains.

Lesson learned.

The brisk wind blew through his coat—the coat that had kept him plenty warm during the past three winters in Dallas—and pricked his skin like shards of ice. Snow stung his cheeks and collected on his eyelashes as he made his way across the parking lot to The Summit bar.

When he'd arrived yesterday he'd thought the snow was sort of cool. The way it covered every available surface, all pristine white and fluffy, made the town look like a postcard. Or one of those snow globes his aunt Rita collected.

But still, enough was enough already. How did people live with this all winter?

Thank God he had no plans to stay in town longer than a few weeks. That is, if all went according to plan.

He opened the door, stepped inside the warm building and took off his Stetson, hitting it against his thigh to dislodge the snow. He scanned the bar, noting the exits, plus a short hallway and swinging doors that must lead to the kitchen. A guy with a shock of wiry gray hair nursed a beer at the end of the bar. A couple of college-age kids were shooting pool, while three men in suits sat at a table by the jukebox, stretching their lunch hour into two. Or three.

A sharp-featured redhead in snug blue jeans and a long-sleeved black T-shirt, carrying a bottle of wine in each hand, pushed through the swinging doors. With her short, spiky hair and slim figure, she deserved the second look the college kids gave her.

Dean walked up to the bar. "Allison Martin?"

"Sorry to disappoint, but I'm not Allie," she said over her shoulder as she set the bottles with the rest of the stock in front of a large mirror. "I'm Kelsey Martin." She took one look at him, her green eyes shrewd, and grinned. "But don't worry, if you're straight, you'll get over any disappointment real quick once you meet Allie."

He blinked. *If* he was straight?

He switched his hat to his other hand. "I'm Dean Garret. I—"

"Hold that thought," she said, before crossing to the cash register, where one of the businessmen waited.

Dean drummed his fingers on the scarred wood, realized he was doing so, then stopped. He set his hat on the bar and studied her as she swiped a credit card through the machine. How should he play this? Over the past two years he'd had a number of jobs, each of which had required him to be an excellent judge of people.

A trait he used to his advantage as often as possible.

He jerked the zipper of his jacket down while Kelsey sent her customer off with a friendly goodbye. When she'd spoken to him, there'd been no personal interest or attraction in Kelsey Martin's eyes, so he'd save his patented I'm-just-a-good-ole-boy-from-Texas routine for the one woman who mattered to him.

"Sorry about that," Kelsey said. "You're looking for Allie?"

"She's expecting me."

"With Allie, that's debatable."

He frowned. "Sorry?"

"Sometimes…well…time gets away from her." The guy at the end of the bar raised his empty glass and Kelsey nodded at him. She pulled a draft and indicated the swinging doors with her head. "Allie's in the kitchen. You can go on back."

He picked up his hat and circled the bar. Opening one door a few inches, he heard the synthesized sound of a syrupy pop song. *Great*. He had a few simple rules, lines he didn't cross. He didn't cheat. He kept to the truth as much as possible. He didn't get personally involved with the people he worked with.

And he didn't listen to crappy music or even pretend to like it.

After all, a man had to have his standards.

He stepped into the large, industrial kitchen. She stood at the stove, her back to him, wearing a fuzzy, deep purple sweater that slid off her shoulder '80s style, as well as black, pointy heeled, knee-high boots and a leather miniskirt. Her dark, straight hair was pulled into a high ponytail but still fell to the middle of her back, and when she did a little shimmy, it took him a moment to realize the harmonizing tones weren't coming from the radio. They were coming from her.

He clenched his fingers, bending the rim of his favorite hat.

Turning, she spotted him and took a step back. Then flipped the radio off. "Is that a real cowboy hat or just for show?"

"Excuse me?"

"Your hat. Real or no?"

He stared at the hat in question. "Real as it gets."

She clapped her hands together. "Am I imagining it or do I hear a hint of Texas twang?"

"I don't have a…a twang," he muttered. A twang was the nasal sound his youngest brother made when he tried to sing along with Brooks and Dunn. What Dean had was an accent that he could downplay or exaggerate depending on the situation.

"No offense," she said offhandedly. "I'm just so excited because you're exactly what I need."

"I'm Dean Garret," he said smoothly. "We have an interview? For the bartending job?"

She waved her hand in the air. "Yeah, yeah. We'll get to that, but first we have something more important to figure out." She glanced over her shoulder. "Just set your coat on the chair there."

Shrugging out of the garment, he laid it on the back of the chair, and crossed the room. "Ma'am, I'm not sure I—"

She shoved a triangle of quesadilla into his mouth. "What do you think of this?"

Since he had no choice, he chewed. It didn't taste like any quesadilla he'd ever had before. And for the life of him he couldn't figure out what she'd put in it—not shrimp or crab. Then, out of nowhere, the heat hit him.

His throat burned; his mouth felt as if he'd just chowed down on a fireball.

"I tried to get Kelsey's take on it but she wouldn't try it because it has tomatoes. Isn't that the craziest thing you ever heard? Who doesn't like tomatoes?"

His face flushed and sweat formed on his upper lip.

"I mean," Allison continued, "she eats pizza and pasta sauce—both of which, I shouldn't have to point out, are tomato based." The woman paused long enough to take a breath. "Well?"

He cleared his raw throat. "How much hot sauce did you use?" he wheezed.

Her eyebrows drew together. "Did I add too much? The recipe called for four tablespoons, but I got called away in the middle of making it and couldn't remember… I figured another tablespoon or two couldn't hurt, right?"

"You thought wrong."

"Are you sure?"

"I'm sure," he said. "Didn't you try it?"

She wrinkled her nose. "I don't like spicy food, which is why I needed an opinion." She smiled, and it was like being struck by a bolt of lightning. "But maybe

I should get a second one. Opinion, that is. Just in case you're like me and can't handle a little heat."

He scowled. Which he knew was damn intimidating—especially when combined with his size. Even with her high heels, he had a good five inches on her.

"Lady," he growled, "I can handle spicy food. That—" he jabbed a finger at the offending quesadilla "—isn't a little heat. It's a blowtorch. My lips are still tingling."

She burst out laughing.

Women. He'd spent a good deal of his life studying them, but he'd learned only one thing for sure.

They never did what you expected.

THE BIG COWBOY BRISTLED, but his hooded eyes gave none of his thoughts away. Allie swallowed the rest of her laughter. Some guys just had no sense of humor.

Too bad. He was seriously cute though, with his sandy-blond hair and aquamarine eyes. Cute in an earthy, masculine, too large and with-a-heavy-dose-of-ride-'em-cowgirl way.

She preferred dark-haired guys who dressed more conservatively than jeans and a striped, button-down shirt.

He picked at the top layer of the remaining quesadilla on the plate. "What's in this, anyway?"

She turned her grill pan off. "Hot sauce—"

"Obviously."

"Tomatoes, some lime juice, onion, scallions…" She ticked each item off on her fingers as she spoke. "Cheddar cheese, cream cheese and lobster."

He jerked his hand back. "Lobster?"

She stirred the big pot of tomato sauce simmering on the back burner. "Sure. Why not?"

He scratched his cheek. "I've never heard of a lobster quesadilla before, that's all."

"That's why I made it. I wanted something different."

"It's different all right," he murmured in his sexy drawl.

She tapped the spoon twice on the edge of the saucepan. It didn't matter what this…cowboy thought about her menu. The Summit belonged to her and if she wanted to liven things up with fancier fare, then she would.

Besides, if she had to cook one more boring cheese-chicken-and-mushroom quesadilla for the next Tex-Mex Monday, she'd stick a fork in her eye.

She slid the band off her heavy ponytail and combed her fingers through her hair. "Well, let's get on with your interview. Why don't we sit down?"

He pulled a chair out for her at the small table. She thanked him and took her seat. Studied him as he sat opposite. Okay, so he was polite. She couldn't help it if she had a weak spot for courteous manners.

She flicked her hair over her shoulder again as she picked up the file containing Dean Garret's résumé, as well as the job application he'd sent in.

"So, I guess we'll get right to the basics," she said. "I need someone to tend bar in the evenings from seven to three Tuesday through Saturday. We're closed Sundays…except during football season."

"Football's big here?"

"We have our fair share of fans. Although if I had to guess, I'd say we're packed Sunday afternoons because people go a little stir-crazy around here in the winter.

They need to get out, and since social opportunities are limited to church functions or skiing, they wind up here."

He leaned forward. "Please tell me there are other things to do in this town beside church dinners and going a hundred twenty miles per hour down a hill on a pair of toothpicks."

"I take it you're not into religion or winter sports?"

He glanced around as if checking to make sure they were alone in the room. "If my mama happens to ask, I attend church every Sunday."

He was afraid of his mama. God, that was sweet. "So it's just skiing you have a problem with?"

"I prefer warmer activities."

Her mouth went dry.

Oh, this wasn't good.

She got to her feet. And about fell back to her seat when he stood, as well. Yeah, those manners were mighty impressive. She went to the refrigerator. "Most guys avoid the ice rink—except for the Tuesday and Thursday night hockey league. And since we're on Main Street, we don't get any snowmobilers coming in, either. They all stop at The Pineview on the edge of town." She opened the fridge door and pulled out a diet soda. "Can I get you something to drink?"

"No, thank you, ma'am." He glanced out the window at the falling snow—and she could've sworn she saw him shudder. "Is there anything to do here that doesn't involve the threat of hypothermia?"

She couldn't help but grin. "Not too much. At least, not between the months of November and February." She pursed her lips as she opened the can. "And sometimes

March." He winced, but covered it quickly. She sat back down and he did, too. "Since you're not a fan of cold weather, I have to ask—are you staying in Serenity Springs long?"

He leaned back, the picture of relaxed, confident male. "I don't plan on leaving anytime soon."

Talk about a nonanswer. "I need someone I can rely on. I've been through too many bartenders to count." He just nodded—in agreement? Pity? Who knew? "To be honest," she continued, "it's getting really annoying to hire someone, only to have them walk away a few weeks—or in one case hours—later. I need someone dependable who's not going to leave me in the lurch."

She sipped her soda and waited, but he didn't say anything. And the intense way he studied her made her squirm.

She cleared her throat. "Now, that's not to say if I hire you I expect you to stay forever…." The idea of staying at The Summit forever caused a chill to run up her spine. "But," she continued, shoving aside the uneasiness she always felt when she thought of her future, "I would appreciate at least two weeks' notice, not to mention a few months worth of work first."

He remained silent.

She sighed. Why were good-looking men always such a trial? "I'm not sure if you understand how a conversation works, but that would be your cue to speak."

He hesitated. Her experience as a defense attorney told her he was readying a lie. But when she searched his expression, she saw no hint of deception.

Which just went to show she'd made the right decision to quit practicing law. She obviously wasn't as good at reading people as she'd thought.

"I'll be in Serenity Springs for a while," he said. "But I can't guarantee how long."

"If I hire you, I need to know you won't leave me in a bind."

Still no response. He didn't try to persuade her he was best for the job, didn't promise he'd stick it out as long as possible. He sure didn't seem all that desperate for work. So why was he here?

She glanced over his résumé again. After graduating from Athens high school in Texas, Dean had worked at a Dallas establishment called Benedict's Bar and Grill for three years before joining the Marine Corps, after which he'd served in both Afghanistan and Iraq. "I see you tended bar before you went into the military, but your recent work record has quite a few gaps. Care to explain those?"

"I was trying to find something that suited."

"Since you're here, I take it you didn't find what you were looking for?"

"No, ma'am."

She picked up a pen and tapped it against the table. "See, this is where we get back to me being able to rely on you to stick around. And from what I can tell of your work history—or at least, your work history over the last two years—you don't stay in one place long."

He clasped his hands together on the table. "After my discharge I did some traveling. For personal reasons."

"Hmm…" He was hiding something. She could feel it. "So you had a difficult time adjusting back to…what would you call it…civilian life?"

"No more than anyone else who served."

She tucked her hair behind her ear and studied him. Maybe he suffered from post-traumatic stress disorder. She was far from an expert on PTSD, but knew that a person affected by it could have trouble keeping a job. Or it could be something else. Wanderlust. The inability to get along with his employers or fellow employees.

And then it hit her why he was so secretive. Why he gave such vague answers. Why there were periods of up to three months unaccounted for in his work history.

"Have you ever been convicted of a criminal offense?"

He raised his eyebrows. "Excuse me?"

"The gaps. I'm just wondering…"

"Are you asking if I was in prison? Is that even legal?"

"In New York State, a prospective employer may ask if a prospective employee has been convicted of a criminal offense, just not if they've ever been arrested or charged with a crime."

Something flashed in his eyes, something like respect. But before she could be certain, he said, "That makes no sense."

"That's the law for you. Besides, being arrested or charged with a crime in no way means you were convicted of said crime."

"You could always run a background check on me."

She sipped her soda. "I could—after I informed you of that fact, of course. But I like to form my own impressions of the people I hire based on what I see and hear from them. Not what the state of New York tells me."

"Would you refuse to hire me if I had a criminal past?"

"Article 23-A of the New York Correction Law prohibits employers from denying an applicant employment because the applicant was previously convicted of one or more criminal offenses." She caught herself and shook her head. She wasn't a lawyer anymore. No need to talk like one. "I just mean that it's illegal, not to mention unethical, to refuse to hire you because of your past. So no, that wouldn't be a problem." She paused. "But you lying about it would be."

"You make a habit of hiring convicted criminals?" he asked, his accent so sexy it made her want to do whatever it took to keep him talking. She tilted her head in a silent question. "Just wondering what type of people I'll be working with if I get the job," he explained.

She took a long drink. "*If* you get the job, you can be assured that none of your coworkers have a criminal record."

After all, Kelsey's juvenile record didn't count, and while Allie's kitchen assistant, Richie, had some past troubles with drug use, he'd never been formally charged with possession.

And Allie's sins hadn't landed her in jail.

Just her own purgatory.

"But," she continued when Dean remained silent, "if you have a problem with people who've paid their dues to society, reconsider if you want this job." And really, did she want someone so…judgmental working for her? "One of my good friends spent time in prison and he stops by quite often."

Dillon Ward, Kelsey's brother, had served time for manslaughter after killing their stepfather while protecting Kelsey. After his release, Dillon had battled prejudice and his own guilt. Luckily, he'd gotten past all of that and was now able to move forward in a relationship with local bakery owner Nina Carlson.

Allie smiled sweetly. "I wouldn't want any of his criminal tendencies to rub off on you."

"You don't have any problems with his past?"

"No," she snapped. She inhaled a calming breath. "I don't have a problem with anyone's past." Well, except her own—but that was what she was doing here, right? Her penance. "I have a bigger problem with people in the present. Out of the last three individuals I hired, one stole from me, one walked off the job and one…" Allie squeezed the can she was holding, denting the aluminum. "She was the worst of all. She lied."

"Lying pissed you off more than desertion and theft?"

"Deserters can come back," she said coolly. "A thief can return what he or she stole. But a liar? You can never take back a lie."

He inclined his head and slowly straightened. "I've never been imprisoned or convicted of a crime."

"And the gaps in your résumé?"

"As I said, I was traveling."

All the signs, everything she'd ever learned about being able to tell when someone was lying, said that Dean Garret was just what he appeared to be. Easygoing. Stoic. Confident. A sexy cowboy in need of a job. If he could mix drinks, he'd be an asset behind her bar. Once word got around about him, women would flock to The Summit just to hear his Texas drawl. And he wasn't so pretty as to put her male patrons on the defensive.

"I guess that's all the information I need then." She

stood, and couldn't help but second-guess herself when he got to his feet, as well. Who knew manners could be such a turn-on? Still, she walked around the table and offered him her hand. "Thank you for coming in."

His large, rough fingers engulfed hers, and damn if a crackle of electricity didn't seem to shoot up her arm and jump-start her heart.

"When can I expect to hear from you?" he asked, still holding her hand.

She pulled free of his grasp and stepped back. "I'm sorry, but you won't."

"I don't understand," he said.

"Listen, I have to be honest. I'm going in a different direction." She met his eyes and told him what her instincts were screaming. "You're just not what I'm looking for."

CHAPTER TWO

DEAN DIDN'T SO MUCH AS blink. Hell, he was so stunned, he didn't even move.

He wasn't what she was looking for? What did that mean? His blood began a slow simmer. Damn it, he was perfect for this job. He'd worked for three years tending bar before joining up. What more did she want? A note from his mother?

"If anything changes," she said, the hint of pity in her tone causing him to grind his teeth together, "I'll be sure to let you know."

In other words, here's your hat, get your ass moving.

He forced himself to smile. "I appreciate your time." He pulled his coat on and set his Stetson on his head. Though his better sense told him not to, he stepped forward until she had to tilt her head back to maintain eye contact. Until her flowery scent filled his nostrils. "You be sure to let me know if you change your mind," he said, letting his accent flow as thick as honey.

Heat flashed in her eyes, turning them a deep, denim blue.

He tipped his hat. "I'll find my own way out."

He didn't slow until he'd pushed open the door and

stepped out into the blowing snow and mind-numbing cold. He trudged across the parking lot, unlocked his truck and slid inside.

He didn't get the job? He slapped his hand against the steering wheel. Unreal. He always got the job. Always got the job done.

He started the engine and cranked up the heat. Allison hadn't believed he'd stay in Serenity Springs.

She didn't trust him.

He sat there, resting his forearms on the steering wheel, and stared at the swirling white flakes drifting down. His record of success was a direct result of his tenacity. He'd go back to his hotel room and regroup. Come up with a plan to somehow convince her he was the best candidate for the job.

That she could trust him.

Even if she really shouldn't.

"YOU SENT HIM PACKING?" Kelsey asked. "But I wanted to keep him. I've never had a cowboy of my very own before."

Allie, perched on the top rung of the stepladder, snorted down at her sister-in-law. "You can't have one now, either." She climbed down, careful to keep her high heels from hooking on the rungs. Once both feet were safely on the ground, she moved the ladder next to the bar. "I don't think Jack would appreciate you wanting to keep this—or any—cowboy."

They were the only people in the bar. Allie hated this time of day—what Kelsey referred to as the dead zone.

The two hours in the afternoon after the lunch crowd left and before people got off work.

Allie knew she should be taking advantage of this lull to get caught up on the pile of paperwork on her cluttered desk. She had inventory sheets to go over. Bills to pay. Taxes to file. Liquor deliveries to schedule and grocery orders to submit.

All of which bored her to tears.

"I guess you're right," Kelsey said in mock disappointment, as if she wasn't completely gaga over Allie's brother, ever since the day they'd met, right here at The Summit a few months ago. Kelsey tapped her forefinger against her bottom lip. "Hey, I know. What if I slap one of those cowboy hats on the sheriff? And do you think spurs would be too kinky?"

"Eww. I think my brain just imploded. And if it didn't, I wish it would." Allie climbed two more rungs and reached down for the red paper heart Kelsey held up to her. "For one thing," she said, hanging the heart from a rafter, "could you please refer to my brother by his name? Or better yet, pick a better nickname for him. He's the police chief, and you calling him 'sheriff' is too weird. What about 'pooky bear'? Or 'snookums'?"

"You expect me to get down and dirty with a man called snookums?" Kelsey grimaced. "That is just wrong."

Allie glared down at her. "And that's the other thing. I don't want to hear anything about you and Jack playing dress up or getting down. Dirty or not. How would you like it if Nina told you all about her and Dillon's love life?"

Nina, a mutual friend, had been involved with Dillon

since Christmas. Everyone around Allie had paired up. It was like Noah's ark.

With her all by her lonesome on a life raft.

Good thing that's how she wanted it, or else she'd be depressed as hell.

Kelsey waved another paper heart in the air. "Nina's far too sweet to ever discuss something like that."

Allie rolled her eyes and descended the ladder. She reached the last rung and slipped, twisting her ankle when she landed on the floor. "Ouch." She rubbed the sore spot through her boot. "Why don't you be a real friend and hang the rest of the decorations?"

"Take your boots off. Why are you climbing a ladder in that getup?"

"Because I don't have any other shoes with me. And if you think I'd walk around in here in my stocking feet, you're more delusional than usual."

Kelsey picked up the ladder and moved it to the end of the bar. "There. I helped. But I'm not hanging any froufrou hearts. You know how I feel about decorating for holidays. Especially ones as commercial as Valentine's Day."

What could Allie say? That she needed to keep busy? That if she stopped for even a minute she started questioning herself? Started wondering if she should've listened to Evan, her ex-boyfriend, and accepted the partnership at Hanley, Barcroft, Blaisdell and Littleton. Or if her life would've been different if she'd never taken Miles Addison's case.

But she had taken it. And she'd been so determined to get ahead that she forgot all the reasons she became a defense attorney in the first place—to help people. People who needed it.

See why she hated this time of day?

"Hey," Kelsey said, rubbing Allie's arm. "You okay? Your ankle isn't sprained, is it?"

Allison rotated her foot while she cleared her thoughts. "No. It's fine. I just can't believe you don't like Valentine's Day, that's all." She climbed the ladder again. She was so counting this as her workout for the day. "Are you sure you're female?"

"Valentine's Day is a holiday made by the greeting card companies and retailers to trick poor saps into spending money on a bunch of useless crap." Kelsey's voice rose and she began to pace. "I mean, what's up with sending flowers? They just die. And if I want candy, I'll pick up a Hershey's bar at the convenience store."

Allie hung a set of pink hearts and climbed down. "What about jewelry?"

She sneered. "Do I look like someone who wants diamonds?"

No, she didn't. Well, except for that gorgeous engagement ring Allie had helped her brother pick out. "You poor thing," she said, wrapping an arm around Kelsey's stiff shoulders. "Have you ever gotten a valentine?"

"I never wanted one," Kelsey said haughtily.

"I'm sure Jack will get you something superromantic," Allie assured her. She gave Kelsey a little squeeze.

"He'd better," she mumbled. "And it better be expensive."

"At least now I understand why you want to host a

speed-dating event on Valentine's Day. You're rebelling against romance."

Kelsey crossed her arms. "I'm all for romance. The speed dating thing gives our customers a chance to find true love. And if they happen to find love while helping our bottom line, all the better."

Allie grinned and folded the ladder before carrying it back down the hallway to the supply closet. Her good humor faded as she realized what had become of her life. Instead of playing a very important part in the American legal system, she now spent her time hanging cheap decorations, preparing the same meals over and over, and avoiding paperwork.

She slammed the closet door shut. Well, she'd wanted to change her life. As usual, when she set out to do something, she'd succeeded. And while running a bar might not be as exciting as practicing criminal law, it was a lot less stressful.

And she wasn't unhappy, she told herself as she went into the kitchen. She loved Serenity Springs and had fabulous friends and the best, most supportive family a person could ask for. A family that didn't ask too many questions. Such as why she'd quit her job and moved back.

She owned her own business, which was growing by leaps and bounds. Plus, she got to do something she enjoyed every day. Even if a year ago she hadn't considered her love of cooking to be anything other than a fun hobby.

Hey, she was nothing if not adaptable.

She gave her pasta sauce a quick stir, adjusted the flame under the pot and picked up her coat.

"I'm going home to change," she told Kelsey as she walked back into the bar. "The sauce is simmering, so could you check it once or twice? Oh, and I almost forgot, can you switch the appetizer on the specials board to grilled flat bread pizza? I'll do a veggie one and a chicken one."

Kelsey leaned against the bar and sipped from a bottle of water. "Sure. But hey, before you go, you never told me why you did it?"

"We've offered bruschetta twice this month," Allie said, pulling on her red leather coat, "and it hasn't gone over too well. I thought we'd try something different."

"No, why did you reject Mr. Tall, Not-So-Dark but Very Handsome? Didn't he pass your test?"

Well, damn. And here she thought she'd avoided the subject of Dean Garret.

"Actually," Allie said, lifting her hair out from beneath her coat, "he passed with flying colors. He didn't hit on me once."

Although she remembered how, right before he left, he'd stepped closer to her, how his eyes had heated and his voice had lowered.

Kelsey set her glass on the counter and crossed her arms. "If he passed the test, what was the problem?"

Allie shrugged and picked up her purse. "He wasn't right for The Summit."

"Ahh." She nodded sagely. "In other words, he didn't need to be saved."

Allie narrowed her eyes. "What's that supposed to mean?"

"You only hire the downtrodden, the needy or, in a

few memorable cases, the just plain pathetic. You're like the Statue of Liberty. All you need is a tattoo on your forehead that reads 'Give me your poor, your tired, your flakes who don't know the difference between a cosmo and a mojito....'"

"So?" Allie asked, sounding to her own ears suspiciously like a pissy teenager. "I don't know the difference between them, either."

"Which is why you need to hire a bartender who does. Besides, none of the people you've hired since I've been here have stuck around. What does that tell you?"

Allie pulled on her black leather gloves. "That my manager keeps firing them all?"

"Hey, I only fired three of them—and they all deserved it. The rest quit. And they quit," she continued, when Allie opened her mouth to speak, "because though you tried to save them from themselves, they weren't interested. All they wanted was to get on with their dysfunctional lives."

"Who was stopping them?" Allie zipped her coat. "You act like I offered counseling sessions as part of a benefits package or something."

"Pretty close," Kelsey mumbled.

"Relax. I'm telling you, Dean Garret isn't right for this job. Trust me on this, I'm doing the right thing here."

"I hope so," Kelsey called after her as Allie walked out the door.

She shivered and hurried over to her car. Yeah, she hoped so, too. And Kelsey was way off base about her trying to save people. She was out of that game.

Because the last time she'd played, she'd saved the wrong person.

THE NEXT DAY, Dean held his cell phone between his shoulder and ear as he dropped a cardboard pizza box onto his motel bed. "Hey there, darlin'," he said when his call was picked up, "it's me. I need a favor."

"I'm not that kind of girl," Detective Katherine Montgomery said in her flat, look-at-me-wrong-and-I'll-kick-your-sorry-ass New York accent. And people thought he sounded funny. "And don't call me darlin'."

The corner of his mouth kicked up. He'd met Katherine over a year ago when he'd worked in Manhattan. The mother of three teenagers, she'd been married for twenty-five years and was built like a rodeo barrel. She was also one of the most savvy cops working in the anticrime computer network in the NYPD, and she didn't take crap from anyone—least of all him.

Was it any wonder he was half in love with her?

"Now don't be that way," he said, flipping the box open and sliding a piece of pepperoni-and-onion pizza onto a paper towel. "I'm betting with the right incentive, you could be talked into being that kind of girl."

He could almost see her scowling at the phone as she sat behind her very tidy desk. "If you keep up with the sweet talk, my husband's going to hunt you down," she warned.

Her husband, a skinny, balding postal worker, wasn't much of a threat and they both knew it. Unless the guy attempted to whack Dean upside the head with his mailbag. "For you, I'd risk it."

"Uh-huh." She made a soft slurping sound—probably sipping her ever-present coffee—before saying, "So you called me two hours before quitting time on a Friday afternoon in another pathetic attempt to sweep me off my feet?"

"Well, that wasn't the only reason." Dean bit into his pizza, chewed and swallowed before wiping his hand on his jeans. He slid his notebook toward him and flipped it open. "I need everything you can give me about a Terri—*T-e-r-r-i*—Long." He gave her Terri's social security number, date of birth and last known address. "I need everything you can find, the more personal the better."

"And you think I'm going to help you why?"

Dean took another bite of pizza and popped the top of a can of soda. "Because it'd take me at least three days to find out even a quarter of what you could discover in a few hours?"

"Yeah. That'd be why." She repeated back to him the information he'd given her. "Who's Terri Long?"

He finished his pizza. "At the moment she's my competition for a bartending job I'm interested in."

"Do I even want to know why you want a bartending job?"

"Probably not."

"Uh-huh." He heard the distinct sound of Katherine tapping at her keyboard. "You're not doing anything illegal, are you, Dean?"

"Not at the moment."

Silence filled the line. "What did you do?"

"Nothing." He switched the phone to his other ear. "Nothing you need to know about, anyway."

Like how he'd broken into The Summit last night and

gone through Allison Martin's office until he'd discovered the name of the person she'd given his job to.

Technically, yes, breaking and entering was illegal. But he hadn't stolen anything.

Other than information, that is.

And most importantly, he hadn't been caught. In Dean's book, that meant he hadn't done anything wrong.

"If you get hauled off to jail again," Katherine warned him quietly, "don't even think about calling me. Especially if you're more than one hundred miles away from Manhattan."

"Now, you know how much I appreciated you flying down to Atlanta to bail me out. Didn't you get the gift basket I sent you?"

Katherine grunted. He would've been worried if he hadn't still heard her typing. "Next time you send me fancy chocolates, send them to the station. By the time I got home, Mickey and the kids had already eaten half the box."

"You got it." He lifted his hips, pulled his wallet from his back pocket and took out his credit card. As soon as he got off the phone with Katherine, he'd call the chocolate shop.

"Want me to e-mail you what I find?"

"That'll do. And thanks. I owe you one."

"You owe me at least a dozen. But who's counting?" Katherine asked with a sigh. "Just promise you'll be careful."

"Always."

He disconnected the phone and tossed it aside. Allison Martin needed his help to realize she'd hired the wrong person. Now all he had to do was sit back and wait for Katherine to work her magic. Then he'd make his next move.

He shot his crumbled paper towel into the garbage can in the corner. Once he had the job, once he had her trust, it was simply a matter of time before everything else fell into place for him.

He'd make damn sure of it.

BEING SURROUNDED BY barely dressed coeds sure made a woman feel every single one of her almost thirty-two years.

Allie drew a beer and handed it to her customer, a fully dressed, beefy kid of twenty-two. "Here ya go," she told him with a grin.

Hey, she could flirt with younger guys just as easily as men her own age. And if she gave some kid a thrill by smiling at him, who was she hurting? In the dim light of the bar she noticed him blush all the way to the dark blond roots of his crew cut. He stammered a thank-you as he hurried off.

See? She was just doing her best to spread a bit of sunshine wherever she went.

Allie turned her attention back to her lineup of thirsty customers. A brunette in a bright pink tube top sauntered to the horseshoe-shaped bar in her three-inch sandals.

Someone needed to tell these kids that it may be called spring break, but that didn't mean they should dress as if they were in Florida. For God's sake, it was ten degrees outside.

Dear Lord, she'd sounded like her mother. And had

called her customers—most of whom were barely ten years younger than her—kids.

She might as well start wearing support hose and let her hair go gray.

"Two cosmos and a strawberry margarita," the brunette said over the blaring jukebox and loud voices.

"Coming up." Allie poured the margarita ingredients into a clean blender and added a scoop of ice. With the machine whirring, she then worked on the cosmos. After making at least a dozen tonight, she didn't even have to consult the cocktail book Kelsey had given her.

Go her. If she didn't have another, oh, twenty or so people wanting drinks, Allie would take the time to pat herself on the back.

Too bad memorizing the ingredients in a few select drinks was about the only thing that had gone right tonight. After a small Saturday night dinner crowd, The Summit had been inundated with college kids ready to party. The sight of her bar packed wall to wall with customers had made Allison's heart go pitter pat.

Until Terri Long called five minutes before her shift was to start to say she wouldn't be coming to work for Allie, after all. Seemed she had a shot at the big time— whatever that meant—and wasn't even in Serenity Springs anymore.

Allie viciously shook her cosmo ingredients and filled two glasses. She hoped there was a special place in hell for people who blew off work.

That was the last time she'd ever hire someone without checking references.

She tossed straws into the cosmos and poured the

margarita into a glass. She sent tube-top girl on her way and began filling the next order as the too-familiar opening chords of "Hotel California" came on the jukebox. Allie gritted her teeth. No doubt about it. This was not her night.

She finished the drinks and recorded the sale on the register. At least her male customers were easy to please. A smile or flip of her hair and they were falling all over themselves to charm her. Even after waiting in line for a solid fifteen to twenty minutes to get a beer. She just thanked God all they wanted to drink was either beer, shots or the occasional rum and coke.

Noreen, her very grumpy middle-aged waitress, was keeping beer pitchers full and the rowdiest customers in line.

Allie glanced at the door, where Luke Ericson was perched on a stool, a grin on his too-handsome face as one of the three girls surrounding him whispered in his ear. When he'd walked in an hour ago, Allie had given him free drinks for the night in exchange for him checking IDs at the door.

None of that made up for the fact that her feet were killing her, she had a huge cranberry juice stain on the front of her favorite jeans and she was starting to wonder if she was breaking a fire code with so many people in the place.

She stepped back toward the line of customers, but stopped when something at the far end of the bar caught her eye.

Her heart thumped heavily in her chest—once, twice, before it found a quick rhythm. Well. Her night might be getting better, after all.

"You must've found something in town to keep your interest," she called over to Dean.

"How do you figure?"

She crossed to him. "You're still here."

"I'm heading out tomorrow. Got a job in Saranac Lake."

She kept her smile firmly in place. Well, that's what she got for not hiring him when she'd had the chance. "Congratulations. How about a drink to celebrate?"

"Whatever you have on tap is fine."

She got his beer and took it over to him. When he pulled out his wallet she waved him off. "On the house."

He studied her for a moment before putting his wallet away. "Appreciate it."

For the next half hour, she poured drinks, all the while aware of a pair of aquamarine eyes following her every move. She set a fresh beer in front of Dean—who seemed oblivious to the fact that the three giggling, just-this-side-of-legal girls next to him were vying for his attention.

Sometimes men could be so clueless.

"What can I get you?" Allie asked the girl with the cute pixie haircut.

She slid a look at Dean. "Sex on the Brain."

"Sweetie, sitting next to this guy—" Allie motioned to him "—would give my ninety-two-year-old grand-mother sex on the brain. What drink do you want?"

The girl giggled and leaned on the bar, the better for Dean to have a clear view down her low-cut top. "Sex on the Brain *is* a drink."

Allie glanced at Dean, arching an eyebrow. He nodded. She sighed and brushed her hair back. Well, that figured.

"Could I speak with you for a moment?" Before Dean could answer, she walked around the end of the bar, took him by the arm and pulled him off his stool. "Don't worry, ladies. I'll bring him right back."

He didn't fight her and she easily hustled him behind the bar. "Quick. What's in a Sex on the Brain?"

He scratched his cheek. "Couple of things."

"Okay," she said to no one in particular, "that's it." She wrapped both hands around the lapels of his jacket and yanked him forward. Noted how his eyes widened slightly. "I'm not in the mood for games, so you can drop the laconic cowboy act."

He kept his hands at his sides. Just tilted his head to the side. "What act?"

She growled. "Listen, I'm tired, I have an endless supply of people waiting for drinks and I'm surrounded by about a million overly perky, faux tanned coeds." Allie inhaled, then rushed on when he opened his mouth. "I've had to pull the same girl—intent on show-ing everyone her coyote-ugly act—off the bar not once, but three times, and I've been hit on by just about every guy in here. But the worst thing is I don't know what I'm doing. And I can't call my sister-in-law to come and show me because she caught some nasty stomach bug from my niece. Suffice it to say I'm not in the best of moods." Allie tightened her hold on his jacket and stood on her toes so that her forehead bumped his chin. "So do not even think about messing with me."

"I wouldn't dream of messing with you," he said, his voice husky and somehow intimate.

Oh. She blinked. Pried her fingers open and stepped

back. "Well then." She swallowed. "How do I make a Sex on the Brain?"

"I'll show you." He took off his jacket, and she could've sworn every female in the room sighed. His black T-shirt hugged the smooth planes of his chest and molded to his biceps. The man was beautiful.

Now if only he'd left his hat on, the moment would've been perfect. Allie knew she was going to have some erotic dreams about that hat.

Dean tossed his jacket on a shelf under the bar. "Fill a tall glass with ice."

She set the glass of ice in front of him. He stuck a straw in it and added a shot each of peach schnapps, vodka and Midori melon liqueur. He then laid an upside-down spoon against the glass and slowly poured in pineapple juice, followed by orange juice and then sloe gin, resulting in a drink that resembled a stoplight: green on the bottom, yellow in the middle and red on top.

"You're a genius," Allie declared. "And my personal hero. I'll give you three hundred bucks to work the rest of the night."

She forced herself not to back up when he leaned toward her. "Darlin'," he purred into her ear, his warm breath causing her to shiver. "I thought you'd never ask."

CHAPTER THREE

ALLISON MARTIN DIDN'T know squat about tending bar.

But she sure knew how to work a crowd, Dean thought as he collected empty bottles and carried them to the recycling bin. She'd flirted, socialized and kept her customers happy while they waited for their drinks.

He glanced at her as she cleared tables. They'd had last call twenty minutes ago and after the final drink had been served, she'd turned on the lights and dived into the cleanup with the same get-it-done spirit she'd demonstrated behind the bar.

The owner wasn't afraid to get her hands dirty.

And she was easy on the eyes. Tonight she had on a pair of snug, dark jeans tucked into those same pointy heeled boots she'd worn during his botched interview. Her shirt was the color of cranberries, with a wide, square neck and long, filmy sleeves that billowed out over her wrists.

Dean took the mixers apart to be washed. She'd had every poor sap in the place drooling over her, wishing that somehow, miracle of miracles, she'd end up with him tonight.

"Well, you sure proved me wrong," Allie said as she came behind the bar and set down her full tray.

She'd told him to call her Allie, although he wanted to continue to think of her as Allison. Or better yet, Ms. Martin. He needed to keep as much distance and formality between them as possible. But she didn't make it easy.

He stacked dirty dishes to the left of the three-bay sink. "How so?"

"I should've hired you in the first place." She gave him a pat on the arm, and damn if he didn't want to back up. Out of range. She moved away to empty the garnish tray. "You charmed every girl in here—heck, you even managed to get Noreen to smile, which, believe me, is an accomplishment."

"She was laughing at my suggestion that she stay to help clean up."

"Well, that makes more sense." Allie washed her hands and dried them on a clean towel. "I'm sure she told you cleanup's not part of her job."

He rubbed the back of his wrist over an itch on his forehead, then resettled his hat on his head. For some reason, Allie had asked him to wear it while he worked. "I couldn't repeat what she told me. At least not in mixed company."

Allie waved at a departing customer. "Noreen was one of the very few females in here tonight immune to your charms. And don't think I missed that brunette with the big—" he raised his eyebrows and she grinned "—*lungs* hand you a cocktail napkin. I'm guessing it had her name, phone number and even a hand-drawn heart on there, as well."

He kept his attention on the glasses he was washing. "It wasn't a cocktail napkin," he mumbled.

"I saw her give you something, and it wasn't very big." Allie swept her hair back and put it in a messy, sexy knot at the back of her head. "Please tell me she didn't write her number on toilet paper."

"Not toilet paper, either."

"Come on," she said, swatting him with the towel. "Don't be cruel. I'm too tired to play guessing games."

He pressed his lips together as he rinsed a glass, then cleared his throat. "It was her thong."

Silence filled the room. He glanced at Allie, just to make sure she was still breathing.

Her mouth popped open. "Oh, my God. You're a rock star." Chuckling, she shook her head. "Well, the poor girl was no match against you. You throw out some mighty strong pheromones."

To Dean's everlasting shame, heat climbed his neck. "She was just…friendly."

Allie laughed even harder. "I think it's safe to assume she wanted to show you how friendly she could be. Now I have to ask—did you keep it?"

"I thought it'd make a nice addition to my collection."

"No doubt about that." She poured herself a diet cola. "I hope you washed your hands after touching it."

"Washed them and then stuck them in the disinfectant just to be safe."

Allie picked up her tray. "You don't know how relieved I am to hear that."

He waited until she was out from behind the bar before saying, "And you were right." She stopped and looked at him. "Her name and number were on the thong," he said, "along with a little heart." Which had half amused, half horrified him.

Allie laughed again as she went to finish clearing tables.

Dean lifted his hat long enough to run a wet hand through his hair. He needed to watch himself. She was damn likable, but he couldn't let his guard down.

Allie came back and set her tray on the bar. "So, tell me about this job in Saranac Lake."

She stood on tiptoe and reached for her soda. He caught a brief, tantalizing glimpse of smooth cleavage and a lacy black bra.

He cleared his dry throat. "Tending bar at the Valley Brook Resort. Starts Monday."

"I'm impressed. The Valley Brook is pretty upscale. You must've wowed them with your interview."

"Like I didn't wow you?"

She tapped her fingertip against her glass. "Let's just say I'm used to more…vocal interviewees. You know, people who speak when spoken to."

"Good thing for me the people at Valley Brook didn't have the same problem." He dried his hands and grabbed a bottle of water from the cooler. "Besides, I'm not sure what you've heard, but it's important for bartenders to be good listeners. Not talkers."

She set her glass down with a soft clink. "Well, then you must be a great bartender."

He almost grinned. "I saved your ass tonight, didn't I?"

"That you did. Could you hand me a clean rag so I can wash off the tables?"

He handed her one, making sure he didn't touch her,

then took a long drink before asking, "What happened to the bartender you did hire?"

"Not sure. She seemed excited to get the job, and was even apologetic when she called to tell me she wasn't coming in." Allie shrugged. "Guess she had a better offer."

Yeah. She had. He'd made sure of it. Katherine had found out that Terri Long's real ambition was the stage. She'd followed her boyfriend—a ski instructor—to Serenity Springs. Dean had pulled some strings and got Terri hired as an understudy in an off-, off-Broadway show, effectively ending Terri's desire to work at The Summit.

He wondered if it ended her desire for her boyfriend, as well.

"That's too bad," he said. "Hope you find someone else."

"OKAY, GUYS, NIGHT'S OVER," Allie told the last three men left in the bar. "Last call was forty-five minutes ago. Time for you to move on."

Two of them slid their chairs back, but the dark-haired one in the middle, the biggest one, didn't budge. "I'm not done with my drink," he slurred.

She sighed. Why were the biggest ones always so much trouble? "You've got five minutes to finish it and get on your way. Or else I call the cops to come and escort you out."

"That won't be necessary," the taller, lankier one on the left said, his Adam's apple bouncing as he swallowed. "Right, guys?"

The shorter one with the thick neck nodded, while Big Guy glared at his beer.

"Five minutes," she repeated, walking away.

Since Dean had everything under control behind the bar, she finished wiping off tables. She hated to think about what her night would've been like if he hadn't shown up. Even Noreen had said he wasn't half-bad.

And from Noreen, that was high praise indeed.

Allie scrubbed at a sticky spot on a corner table. She had to admit Dean had impressed her. He'd not only saved her ass—as he so eloquently put it—but he'd stuck around to help clean up. Which meant she might get home and in bed before the sun rose.

Yep, no doubt about it. Dean was her hero. She wiped the table dry before setting the chairs on it. She just had to figure out how she was going to persuade him to give up his job in Saranac Lake and work for her instead.

She ran her hands down her jeans, picked up her rags and headed behind the bar. "You have everything under control back here?"

"So far," Dean said.

He was quite the man of understatement. But during the past few hours she'd come to realize that although he talked slowly and took his time, he was far from stupid or lazy. He got the job done, kept the customers happy and seemed at ease whether trying to sweet-talk Noreen into cleaning, or shutting down a young coed when they'd overimbided.

Hey, maybe there was something to being laid-back.

She'd have to give it a try sometime.

She refilled her glass, drinking from it and then nodding at the three young men getting to their feet. "I'm glad they're leaving. I was afraid I'd have to call Jack."

Dean tipped his hat back. "Jack? That your boyfriend?"

"No, my brother." She ran her finger through the condensation on her glass. "He's also the police chief."

"That's handy."

"It's great," she agreed. "I can always count on him to bail me out. And then lecture me until my eyes cross."

Was it any wonder she'd never told Jack what had happened a year ago, what she'd done, before she'd bought The Summit? Even after all these months she still had a hard time facing herself in the mirror. She didn't need to face her family's disappointment in her, as well.

She bent to tie a bag of garbage closed as the three kids passed the bar. Instead of moseying on out, though, the big one stopped. "I changed my mind." He hefted himself onto a stool and slammed his hand on the bar. "I want another beer before we go."

"Sorry, no can do," Allie said before Dean could respond. "We've already had last call."

"Come on, Harry," his tall buddy said, glancing warily at Dean. "Let's get back to the hotel. We've got a twelve-pack there, remember?"

Harry—did people still name their kids that?—stood and shoved his companion into the bar. "Back off. I want my beer here."

"I'm giving you ten seconds," Allie said, making her voice as cold as the weather outside despite the uneasiness in her stomach, "then I'm calling the cops."

Harry puffed up his chest, swaying with the effort. "I'll go when I'm ready to go."

Both of his friends began talking at once, trying to convince him. Before Allie could pick up the phone to call in the cavalry—namely Jack—Dean sighed and tossed down his cleaning rag. She grabbed his arm.

"What are you doing?" she asked.

He looked at her as if she'd been drinking the disinfectant solution. "I thought I'd convince young Harry and his followers to go home."

"But there are three of them."

He gently peeled her fingers off his arm. "I appreciate your concern, but I think I can handle the Three Stooges here."

Then he walked around the bar. She bent down and picked up the Louisville Slugger Dillon had made her promise to keep under the bar for protection. Her hands shook as she wrapped her fingers around the handle.

If she had to hit someone with this thing she was going to be mighty ticked off.

Dean, in no particular hurry that she could see, sort of...ambled...up to Harry and his friends. The kids flanking Harry took a step back. Must be Dean's sheer size. It couldn't be his fierce demeanor. From what she'd seen of him, the guy was so easygoing she was surprised he didn't slip into a coma.

"You're ready now," Dean said quietly.

Harry held on to the bar as if trying to remain upright. "What?"

"You said you'd go when you were ready. You're ready now."

"Says who?"

Allie blinked. Had she somehow been transported

back to grade school? No, they weren't a couple of ten-year-olds calling each other names. They were two very large, fully grown men facing off in front of her.

Dean kept his hands loose at his sides. "Bar's closed."

"Back off." The guy punctuated his statement by shoving him in the chest.

Dean took a step back to keep his balance, and Allie tightened her grip on the bat, her pulse skittering. But instead of losing his temper, he looked at Harry's friends. "You'd better get your buddy out of here before he lands all of your asses in jail."

Harry sneered. "Why don't you go back to the range or wherever you came from?" He leaned forward and knocked Dean's hat right off his head.

Oh, Harry, that wasn't a smart move.

"Kid," Dean said with a quiet intensity that made her shiver, "you have a lot to learn. The first of which being don't ever touch another man's hat." He stepped forward. The two smarter ones backed up. "Now, you've got two seconds to get your butt out of this establishment—"

"Or what?" Harry asked, with more beer-induced bravado than brains.

Dean actually grinned. A dangerous and—okay, sexy—grin that said please give me an excuse so I can smash your head in.

Not that she blamed him. After all, Harry had knocked his hat off.

"Or else I escort you out personally," Dean said, making no doubt that it wasn't a statement, but a promise.

The two men stared each other down. Tension filled the room; the threat of violence permeated the still air.

Allie cleared her throat. "I hate to interrupt this testos-
terone battle, but do you want me to call the police?"

"That won't be necessary," Dean said, never taking
his attention off the kid. "Will it, Harry?"

"No," Harry grumbled after a moment. His friends,
sensing their chance, took hold of his arms and started
pulling him backward. "This bar sucks, anyway."

She loosened her grasp on the bat. Crisis averted.
Thank God.

Or it was until Harry wrenched free of his friends and
swung wildly at Dean's head.

She gasped and raised the bat to her shoulder, but
Dean didn't need her coming to his rescue. In one
smooth move he stepped to the side, pulled his arm
back and punched Harry. Allie grimaced at the crunching sound of bone hitting bone as Dean's fist connected
with the drunk's nose.

Harry groaned and slid to the floor in a heap.

Allie's palms were so sweaty the bat slipped out of
her grip and hit the floor with a loud bang. But
nobody seemed to notice. Harry's friends stared wide-
eyed at Dean, and Harry...well, poor Harry wasn't
doing anything except bleeding. While Dean stood
there, big and imposing and a little scary, with his
hands clenched.

He then raised an eyebrow at the two friends. They
both shook their heads.

Holy cow. The man was like some Chuck Norris
wannabe. No wonder he'd patted her on the head when
she'd tried to talk him out of confronting Harry and his
buddies. From what she'd just seen, she wouldn't be sur-

prised to find out he could've taken all three of the younger men at the same time.

Her initial reaction to Dean had been right. There was way more to him than met the eye.

Dean snatched up his hat, sat it on his head and knelt next to Harry, who had come to enough to moan. "Another thing you need to learn," he told the kid cheerfully, "is not to start a fight you have no chance of winning."

WHY DID HE ALWAYS GET stuck working with the soft-hearted ones? In the last year he'd done jobs for both an inner city teacher whose students ran all over her, and a youth pastor in a small town who wanted to save the kids in his flock from the fires of hell. Too bad the kids were more concerned with having fun than being saved.

Dean shook his head and picked out two bottles of tequila from the supply closet. Once Harry had come around, Allie had hovered over the kid. She'd given him ice for his swelling and cut nose, asked if he needed some pain reliever. Then she'd spoken in depth to Harry's friends, making sure one of them was sober enough to drive. Luckily, the skinny kid was the desig-nated driver or else she probably would've made Dean play chauffeur.

"Did you have to punch him so hard?" she asked as soon as he came back into the room.

"Next time someone takes a swing at me," he said as he added the tequila to the stock behind the bar, "I'll politely ask him to stop."

She crossed her arms. "I just hope he doesn't try and bring you up on charges of aggravated assault. You can claim self-defense, but he might counter that you used excessive—"

"I have a right to protect myself."

"Sounds like you know your law."

"I know my rights," he said, keeping his cool. "You're the one who's talking like a lawyer or something."

She blushed. "That's because I am a lawyer."

Even though he already knew about her past as a defense attorney, he played along. "You're a lawyer and a bar owner?"

"No." She picked up a rag and wiped off the already clean bar. "I…changed careers about a year ago."

He leaned against the counter. "Is your career change working out for you?"

She glanced up at him, a loose strand of hair curved over her cheek. "Oh, yeah. It's been great. Really, really, really great."

Uh-huh. All those *reallys* weren't fooling anyone.

"Were you any good?"

Her eyes grew sad for a moment. "Yeah. I was very good."

He watched her carefully. "Must've been hard to give it up."

The corners of her mouth turned up in a fake smile. "I needed a change."

And if that was the truth, the next time some drunk took a swing at him, Dean would let him connect. "What kind of law did you practice?"

"Criminal. So, I take it you excelled in the marines?"

After a moment's hesitation, he decided to go along with the change in subject. He knew when to let something drop and when to push. Besides, he had plenty of time to get to know Allie. To learn all of her secrets.

Using the broom she'd brought out, he swept behind the bar. "Why do you say that?"

"Uh, because of the way you flattened poor Harry. You must've gotten an A+ at hand-to-hand combat."

"Poor Harry?" Dean shook his head, kept sweeping. "First of all, subduing a drunk civilian doesn't take much skill. Secondly, weren't you the one who wanted poor Harry's butt hauled off to jail?"

She sprayed disinfectant onto the work areas behind the bar. "I wanted to scare him. I didn't realize you were going to go all Walker, Texas Ranger on him."

"I've worked in a lot of bars. Was a bouncer in a few of them and have dealt with plenty of drunken idiots." *True. Sort of.* "And believe me, after a man's been swung at enough times, he'd better be smart enough to learn how to duck. Or how to fight back."

She rolled her eyes. "Now you sound like Jack."

Jack Martin, the police chief brother. And, according to the information Dean had from the cute redhead who worked the desk at the motel, the first Martin sibling to run back to Serenity Springs from New York.

"Jack must be a smart man then," Dean said, picking up the dustpan.

"He is. He's great." She took the broom and swept the dirt into the dustpan he held. "But if he asks, I'll deny I ever said that. As a younger sister, it's my duty to bug, tease and annoy him mercilessly."

"I'll have to call my mother and thank her for not having any daughters."

"You don't know what you're missing."

He dumped the dirt into the trash can. "I have two younger brothers, Ryan and Sam."

"You're from Dallas, right? Is that where they live?"

"Yeah."

"You must miss them."

His fingers tightened on the dustpan's handle. He did miss his brothers. Missed his entire family. It'd been almost two years since he'd walked away from them. But he still couldn't forgive them. Not yet.

And he'd never be able to trust them again. Especially Ryan.

"Looks like we're about finished here." Hey, he could change the subject just as easily as she could. Yes, the best way to get someone to trust you was to pretend to open up to them yourself. But damn, he didn't want to have this particular conversation now.

Or ever.

Besides, the bar was too small, too intimate when they were the only people there, to talk about family. It was too easy to forget he was working.

"Oh. Right. Hold on." She opened the cash register, counted out some money and handed it to him. "I can't thank you enough for helping me."

"Something tells me you would've handled things on your own." He tucked the bills into his pocket.

She stepped closer to him. "What would it take to convince you to give up that job in Saranac Lake and work here instead?"

His heart picked up speed. He loved it when a plan came together.

"Why would I want to do that?"

"Saranac Lake is farther north. It's much colder up there than Serenity Springs." She laid her hand on his arm as she spoke, her fingers warm on his skin. He stood stock-still, his pulse drumming in his ears. His scheme was working almost too well. "Plus, I've been up to the Valley Brook. It's very fancy. You'd have to wear some dorky uniform."

"For what they're going to pay me, I'd wear a clown suit."

She inhaled sharply, as if bracing herself, and took her hand off his arm. "How much did they offer you?"

Since he really didn't have a job offer, he made up a figure he thought was reasonable. But when he told her, she winced. Then she swallowed and lifted her chin. "I'll match it. So what do you say?" she asked hopefully.

When she smiled at him like that, his head buzzed. His hands itched to dive into her thick mass of hair.

Ah, hell. What he was going to do next could lead him into a whole mess of trouble.

It's for the job, he assured himself. To convince her he was just an easygoing cowboy with nothing more on his mind than his next paycheck.

Which was total crap, but he'd hold on to that justification for as long as possible. Because he wanted to touch her, to kiss her before they went any further.

Before there were too many secrets and lies between them.

"I'll accept the job," he said gruffly, "in approximately five minutes."

She laughed. "What? That makes no sense."

"It makes perfect sense." He edged closer to her. She took a step back. Then another, until she was pressed up against the bar. "You see, after I accept the job, you'll be my boss."

"You have a problem with me being your boss?"

"Not at all." He settled his hands on her waist. She tensed, her palms going to his chest. "But once you're my boss, certain…actions on my part would be inappropriate."

"They might be inappropriate even if I'm not your boss."

But she hadn't pushed him away—or hauled off and slapped him.

So he was still in the game.

"They might be." He tugged her warm, lithe body against his, crushing her hands between them. "I need those five minutes." He ignored how true that statement was—and how much it endangered his job—as he pressed his mouth against the rapidly beating pulse at her neck. She gasped. He rubbed his cheek against hers and leaned back so he could look into her eyes. His voice barely a whisper, his mouth hovering over hers, he asked, "What do you say?"

CHAPTER FOUR

ALLIE WANTED TO SET DEAN straight on how things worked at her bar. She was the boss and she didn't go around letting her employees put their hands on her. Or kiss her neck.

Her fingers curled into his chest. He was so warm. Solid.

He slowly lowered his head, but she pushed against him.

His eyes met hers. She blamed her lack of willpower on the intensity in his gaze. How could she worry about mistakes when he seemed so…sexy, yes…but more importantly, so steady?

She slid her palms up to his shoulders. "Okay," she breathed, linking her hands behind his neck and pressing against him.

Finally, his mouth brushed against hers, a featherlight kiss that drove a tingle of awareness and sharp, aching need through her body.

He pulled back and stared down at her. Okay, so curiosity had got the better of them.

No harm done.

She smiled up at him as she stroked the back of his

neck, the silky ends of his just-this-side-of-too-long hair. "We still have at least four minutes left. I think you can do much better than that."

Humor lit his eyes even as they darkened with desire.

And she knew that his desire was real—even while she suspected it was as unwanted for him as it was for her.

Then he kissed her again. He kissed like he'd done everything else so far this evening. Slow. Easy. And with great skill. As if he had all the time in the world to learn the texture of her lips, the taste of her, the way she fit against his body. His tongue swept across the seam of her lips. But not even the rasp of his tongue against hers could break the spell he'd put her under.

She groaned and pressed her breasts against the solid planes of his chest.

He wrapped one arm around her waist and lifted her so that her high heels came off the floor. He slid his other hand into the hair at the nape of her neck, his fingers loosening the knot she'd tied it in as he massaged her scalp, tilted her head and deepened the kiss.

Dear Lord, she hadn't realized one simple kiss could be so…dangerous. To her peace of mind. Her sense of what she could and could not control.

And most importantly, to her willpower.

Then, as if a switch had been flipped, the danger passed. Though he still held her flush against him, she had the sensation of him pulling away. While she would've sworn his earlier kisses had been driven by passion, the touch of his lips on hers now felt…deliberate. Practiced.

Contrived.

She pulled back, breathing hard—definitely harder than a fully clothed, vertical kiss warranted. Allie frowned.

Dean stepped away. His jaw was tight and his chest rose and fell with his own heavy breathing. And while she told herself she was being ridiculous, that like always, she was reading way too much into things, she couldn't help but think there had been something real and honest about what had happened between them when they'd first kissed.

She swallowed and tucked her trembling hands behind her back. "Well, I guess that's it for now."

He nodded. "We could always move our agreement back a few more minutes," he said, his tone serious.

Despite the fact that there was nothing funny about this situation, she laughed. At herself for being such a complete fool. Because even though her instincts were screaming at her not to trust this man, she was tempted to step back into his arms. "I think we'd better stick to our original agreement," she said.

"You're right." He put his jacket on. "When do you want me to start?"

"Tuesday. Your regular shift will start at seven, but I'd rather you come in around six so we can get all your paperwork filled out." She tossed the cleaning rags into the small laundry basket she kept stashed under the bar. "You'll get two fifteen-minute breaks and a half-hour lunch break. All employees get one meal on the house—"

"Free food?"

Funny how her male employees always perked up at that. "Yes, but there are two conditions. One, you eat what's on the menu for that night. There are no special orders."

He nodded solemnly. "Wouldn't want anyone to think this was a restaurant."

What a smart-ass. "It's a restaurant for paying customers, but even for them I have a limited menu. While I enjoy cooking and am glad we can offer lunch and dinners, The Summit is first and foremost a bar."

Or at least, that's what Kelsey kept reminding her.

"What's the second condition?" he asked.

"No complaining about the food. If you don't like my cooking, don't eat it. Bring a bagged lunch or go hungry. I don't care."

"I hadn't realized chefs were so sensitive."

Her face heated and she turned toward the stock in front of the large mirror. "I'm not sensitive," she muttered, rotating bottles so all the labels faced out. "But it's embarrassing to me—not to mention bad for my business—when an employee has pizza delivered, in front of the Friday night dinner crowd, because she thinks my beer-battered fried fish stinks."

He made a choking sound, as if trying to hold back a laugh, but when she glanced at him, his expression was neutral. "I never complain about a free meal. And speaking of meals, since The Summit's not open on Sunday, do you have any recommendations for a good place to eat in town?"

"You don't cook?"

"I can get by. But the motel I'm staying at doesn't even have a minifridge, so I'm limited to takeout until

I can find a place to rent. I'll be glad for any opinions
you have on the local real estate market, too."

"There are usually a few apartments listed in *The
Gazette*," she said. Something kept her from mentioning the newly renovated two-bedroom apartment up-
stairs. "I'm sure you'll be able to find something decent
before too long."

Kelsey had been after Allie for months to rent the
space, but she didn't want the burden of being a landlord.
And since The Summit's income was more than enough
for her to live on, Kelsey didn't push the issue.

And who knew? If Dean stuck around long enough,
they could always discuss his becoming her first
tenant later.

"The Pineview has a terrific Sunday brunch," Allie
continued, "but they close at three. If you're looking for
a good lunch, you can't go wrong with Sweet Suggestions, the bakery on Main Street. Nina's food is great
and reasonably priced. Other than that, I'm afraid your
choices are limited to pizza or burgers." She didn't miss
his quick grimace. "Is that a problem?"

"No. But eating pizza twice a day for three days in a
row makes a man appreciate a home-cooked meal." He
glanced at his watch. "If you're finished, I'll walk you
to your car."

She blinked at the unexpected offer. "Oh. That would
be great. Let me put the cash away and get my things."

She took the drawer out of the cash register and went
down the hall to her office. Tucking the money in her
small safe, she locked it before slipping into her coat and
picking up her gloves and purse. After checking to make

sure the rear door was locked, she hurried back to the bar. Not that Dean seemed in any rush. He was leaning against the wall by the front door, one ankle crossed over the other, his hands in his pockets.

She grabbed her cell phone and stuck it in her coat pocket. "All set," she told him, zipping her coat.

He held the door open for her and they stepped outside into the cold night air. The wind blew her hair into her face as she locked the door. Shivering, she pulled on her gloves.

He flipped up the collar on his coat and hunched his shoulders. "You shouldn't park so far from the building," he said, nodding toward her red SUV at the other end of the snow-covered lot. "Especially since you leave work so late."

"You sound like Jack again." She carefully stepped off the sidewalk, not the least bit surprised when he took her arm so she wouldn't slip. One thing she did trust about Dean Garret—his manners were the real deal. "I usually do, but when I got to work, the guy who takes care of the parking lot for me was plowing, so I had to stay out of his way."

They kept their heads down as they slowly made their way. While her high-heeled boots were stylish, they weren't exactly practical. But Dean, God bless him, didn't comment or try to hurry her along. He just matched his pace to hers.

The wind blew swirls of snow, like little white tornadoes, around them. She stole a glance at Dean's strong profile. There was no doubt about it. He was one sexy cowboy. He was also, she reminded herself, new in town. He didn't have any friends and was staying in a half-rate motel that didn't even have a minifridge. And really, after the way he'd helped her out by pitching in behind the bar, the least she could do was make sure he had a hot meal.

Right?

A few feet from her SUV, she pressed the unlock button on her key ring. Her headlights flashed. He reached for the door and held it open for her.

"Thanks for all your help tonight," she said.

"No problem."

Her teeth chattered. "I guess I'll see you on Tuesday."

He raised his eyebrows. Maybe because her statement had sounded more like a question. Hey, when you go through seven bartenders in eight months, you start to feel a little insecure.

"I'll be there," he said.

"All right then. Good night."

"'Night, boss."

She climbed into her vehicle and he shut the door behind her. She started the ignition, but instead of giving him a polite smile and driving away, she rolled down the window. "You should come over to dinner."

From the look on his face, she'd surprised him as much as she'd surprised herself. "Excuse me?"

"Tomorrow, Sunday dinner," she said, trying to make it sound less crazy than it was. It didn't work, but she wanted credit for trying. "At my parents' house."

"I wouldn't want to bust in on your family dinner."

"We always have room for one more."

He studied her, his expression unreadable in the dim parking lot. "If you're sure…"

"I am. And I'm not saying that because I'm not the one cooking. My mom's always thrilled to have guests."

Although Helen Martin usually preferred a bit of warning about aforementioned extra guests.

He nodded slowly. "I appreciate the invitation."

"Good." She gave him her parents' address. "It's easy to find. Take a right at the corner by the high school— do you know where the high school is?" Another nod, this one quick and jerky. "Go straight two blocks and then take a left onto Pleasant Street. Their house is the first one on the corner. Dinner's at six sharp."

Unable to stand the cold any longer, she rolled her window up, cutting off whatever he'd been about to say. She shifted into Drive and pulled out of the lot. It wasn't until she'd parked in her own driveway that she gave in to the urge to bounce her head off the steering wheel.

She should've kept her big mouth shut. Just because the man was new in town didn't mean she had to be a one-woman welcoming committee.

Besides, even though she'd hired him, even though he seemed like someone she could count on, she didn't trust him.

DEAN'S CELL PHONE RANG. He groaned and blindly reached along the table. His fingers brushed against his phone as it rang again. He flipped it open. "'Lo?"

"Well? Did you get it?"

He covered his eyes with his free arm, blocking out the sunlight filtering through the motel window. "What time is it?"

"Eight o'clock," Nolan Winchester said. "No, I guess

it'd be nine for you. I figured you'd be up by now. And I don't know what the weather's like up there in the Arctic Circle, but here in Dallas it's a gorgeous and sunny sixty degrees already."

"When I get back," Dean muttered to the man who'd been his best friend since they'd met in basic training over ten years ago, "I'm going to kill you. And you can bet it will be painful."

Nolan laughed. Probably because Dean was too tired to put any real heat behind his threat. He'd been too keyed up to sleep when he got back to his motel room, having dozed off sometime after 5:00 a.m.

All because of Allison Martin.

"What do you want?" Dean asked.

"I haven't heard from you since Friday." The sound of kids shrieking made Dean wince and move the phone away from his ear. "Mitchell, put the butter back in the fridge before your sister eats it all."

"You running a circus down there?" Dean asked.

"Feels like it," Nolan said with his usual—and damned irritating—good cheer. "Cassie's sleeping in today and the kids wanted to surprise her with breakfast in bed." One of the three kids—the baby from the sound of it—started bawling. "What's the matter with Daddy's girl?" Nolan asked. The screaming grew louder, more than likely because Nolan had picked Grace up. "Cassie's going to love this delicious breakfast we're making, right, kids?"

Five-year-old Mitchell and three-year-old Ava gave hearty shouts of approval. Dean shook his head. His partner was one lucky guy. He and his high-school sweetheart had recently celebrated their tenth wedding anniversary.

Cassie was, in Dean's mind, about as close as a man could get to the perfect woman. She was a great mother, had a successful career as a real estate agent and hadn't balked when Nolan wanted to move from their hometown in northern Alabama to Dallas to start a business with Dean. Plus, when Nolan had been stationed overseas, Cassie had remained strong and supportive and capable of living on her own.

And she could still fit into her high school cheerleading uniform. A fact Nolan had shared after a few too many beers at the Winchesters' Labor Day picnic.

"So, did you get the job?" Nolan asked.

"Yeah, I got it." Dean sat up and swung his bare feet over the edge of the bed, shivering.

"No kidding?"

"You sound surprised." He pulled the heavy bedspread around his naked shoulders as he got to his feet and went to the heating unit on the wall. He squinted at the blurry numbers then flipped the tiny control as high as it would go. "You underestimating me?"

"Well, you said you'd have to use charm, and I've seen your charm. It's a wonder you ever get laid."

"Daddy," Dean heard Mitchell ask, "what's 'get laid'?"

Dean snorted as he used his teeth to rip open the single-serving bag of coffee.

"Hell," Nolan muttered, hopefully low enough that his kids didn't hear that, as well. "I said it's a wonder Uncle Dean even gets paid."

"No, you didn't," the boy told him.

"Why don't you get the eggs out for me?" Nolan asked.

"Can I crack some?" Dean knew from the kid's tone he was probably bouncing with excitement.

"Me, too!" Another voice, this one Ava's.

"Sure, sure. You can both crack some. But first I need you to watch your baby sister for a minute while I finish talking to Uncle Dean, okay?"

"Cassie's going to kick your sorry ass when she finds out what kind of language you've been using around her babies." Dean filled the coffeepot with water from the bathroom sink.

"Don't I know it." Nolan sounded decidedly less cheerful than when he'd first called. "No sense dwelling, though. Did you find out anything?"

He'd found out that Allison Martin was nothing like he'd expected. He'd also found out The Summit did a fair amount of business and, most surprising of all, people paid money to send their kids to this snow-ridden town to spend spring break—where spring was nowhere to be found.

"I just got the job," Dean pointed out as he poured the water into the coffeemaker and turned it on. "I'm building trust. Playing the part of an easygoing good ole boy."

Sure. And that's what he'd been doing last night. Playing on Allie's trust. Playing his part. Which was the only reason he'd kissed her.

Just doing his job.

"Building trust?" Nolan asked. "You don't have time to build trust. Just find out what you need to know. Ask a few questions, knock a few heads together if you have to—"

"Right there is the reason I do most of the fieldwork while you stay behind and deal with the clients."

He and fellow PI Nolan had formed Leatherneck Investigations when Dean left the service. Though they were still small, their reputation for solving cases—especially missing person cases—had garnered them plenty of business.

"No," Nolan said, "the reason you're there and I'm here is because you won't stay in Dallas more than a week at a time."

Leave it to his partner to get to the heart of the matter.

"Bashing heads won't help us solve this case," Dean said, watching the coffee slowly drip into the pot. "People in small towns think differently. They protect their own. Word gets around I'm asking questions about Allison Martin and any ties she has to a missing persons case, and I'll lose my advantage."

"I still think some well-placed intimidation—oh, hell. Mitchell! Ava! Freeze! Both of you...no...keep your hands where I can see them. Now set the eggs down. Carefully. Mitchell, I mean it. Don't even think about—"

The phone dropped with a loud clang.

Dean grinned. He poured coffee into a hotel mug and took a sip as he crossed back to the bed. He set the cup and phone down and pulled a sweatshirt out of his duffel bag, tugging it over his head. Tucking the phone between his ear and his shoulder, he unplugged his laptop from the charger and turned the computer on.

"Sorry about that," Nolan said breathlessly.

"You're starting to show your age, old man," Dean said, even though he was two years older than his friend.

"Back in the Corps you could run three miles—in full combat gear—in under twenty minutes. Now you're huffing and puffing over corralling your own kids in your kitchen?"

"They're faster than you think. You get that e-mail I sent you? It had the financials you wanted me to check out."

"I'm booting up now." Dean leaned back and picked up the coffee. "Did you find anything?"

"Nothing new. The trail ends in Cincinnati. I still think you would've been better off staying there."

"No point. The lead was dead."

The New York cops had lost Lynne and Jon Addison's trail there, as well. And any interest in the case. According to the detective Dean had spoken with right before he'd headed up to Serenity Springs, the file on the disappearance of Lynne and Jon, the wife and young son of prominent businessman and philanthropist Miles Addison, was still open.

Still open but very much cold.

Now, almost a year later, Dean was trying to pick up the Addisons' trail.

He had very few leads. All he knew for certain was that on a sunny July morning a year and a half ago, Lynne Addison had kissed her husband goodbye before taking their son to the park six blocks away. They hadn't been seen since.

Dean accessed his e-mail account and waited for his new messages to download before opening the attachment and scanning the documents Nolan had sent.

"Damn." He pressed the heels of his hands against

his eyes. He'd been so sure he'd find a clue in Allison Martin's financial records.

"I know you think Allison Martin was involved—"

"She received a call at her office at Hanley, Barcroft, Blaisdell and Littleton from Lynne's cell phone shortly after Lynne and Jon left their residence the day they disappeared."

"Except the call lasted less than five seconds. Ms. Martin claimed there was no one on the other end, so she hung up. No other calls between the women turned up. I still think you're looking in the wrong area. Go back to Cincy, pick—"

"No." Dean closed his laptop and tossed it on the end of the bed. "There are too many coincidences here. First Allison Martin and Lynne Addison are seen having lunch together two weeks before Lynne and her son disappeared—"

"Allison had just saved Miles from a prison sentence," Nolan pointed out. "Lynne probably took her out to thank her."

Two years ago Miles Addison had been accused of sexually assaulting one of the young boys who attended his after-school program for underprivileged youths. Allison Martin had been lead defense counsel on the case, earning an acquittal for the businessman and a prime partnership offer for herself.

"If the meeting was a thank-you lunch, why were they overheard arguing? And according to their waiter, Lynne stormed out before the food was even served." Dean paced the length of the small room. "Add in the phone call the day Lynne and Jon disappeared, and the fact that Allison systematically cleaned out her personal bank account over a period of six months—starting the day before the Addisons disappeared. And considering she had to get a small business loan to purchase The Summit, where did the money go?"

"You're reaching. For all you know she may be an addict and the money was for her dealer."

Dean grabbed a large envelope from the side table and pulled out an eight-by-ten black-and-white photo of Allison. The picture had been taken during Addison's trial, but even dressed in a conservative suit with her hair pulled back there was no denying her sex appeal. He tossed the picture aside. Allison wouldn't be the first bright, driven, successful person to become an addict, but he couldn't picture her using. She had too much confidence and self-awareness to allow something like drugs to control her.

He'd check into it just the same.

"Wherever the money went," he said, "it doesn't explain why, six months after the Addisons disappeared, Allison quit her job and returned to Serenity Springs. I'm telling you, there's something here. I can feel it."

"I'll have to go with you on this one," Nolan said. "But it'd be a lot easier if you could tell Martin that Lynne's mother is looking for her, and ask her straight out if she knows where Lynne and Jon are."

"When have we ever had a case that easy?"

"Never. But I can dream. Then I wouldn't have to deal with Robin Hawley calling twice a day, wondering if we've found anything yet."

Dean's fingers tightened around his phone. "If she'd

believed her daughter about what a scumbag her son-in-law is, instead of testifying for the prick during his trial, maybe she'd still have her daughter in her life."

"You're projecting again. This isn't the same situation you went through with your family."

No, but in the end, both he and Lynne Addison had been betrayed by the people they trusted the most. "Next time Robin calls, tell her to be patient and let us do our job."

"You can't blame her. If what she told us is true, Miles Addison is dangerous. She's terrified he's going to find Lynne before we do. And given the guy's money and connections, she might be right."

Dean stood and stretched his free arm overhead. "Either way, her bugging you isn't going to help us find her daughter and grandson any sooner."

"*If* we find them."

"We will." He couldn't explain how or why he believed that, but he did. Just as he believed he was in the right place being in Serenity Springs. Dean tapped a finger on Allison's picture. "Martin is a solid lead and I'm betting she has information that will steer me right to Lynne and Jon Addison. And I'm not leaving Serenity Springs until I know for sure."

CHAPTER FIVE

"HOW'S THE NEW BARTENDER working out?"

Allie squeaked as she jumped and spun around. She covered her racing heart with her hand for a second before hitting Jack in the arm with a red cloth napkin.

"You're thirty-three years old," she said. "When are you going to stop sneaking up on me?"

He grinned, his blue eyes—so like her own—lit with humor. "When it stops being fun." He set a stack of white dinner plates on the rectangular dining-room table. "Or when you stop jumping and squealing like a girl when I do it."

And therein lay the rub. Jack was surprisingly stealthy for a man his size. She figured it was the cop in him that made him such an expert sneak. Plus, he always managed to catch her daydreaming. Like now.

Just because he'd asked about her new bartender didn't mean he knew she'd been thinking about Dean. Questioning her decision to hire the cowboy. Wondering what he was hiding behind his sexy grin and guarded green eyes.

Her face heated and she ducked her head so that her hair fell forward, hiding the evidence of her blush as she folded napkins.

"Think this one will stick around for more than a few days?" Jack asked.

"'This one'?" Helen Martin asked as she came into the room, carrying a basket filled with silverware.

As usual, their mother looked flawless. She had on a loose tunic the color of a new penny over a pair of khaki corduroy pants. With her dark hair skimming her shoulders in soft waves and her face not really showing many lines, it was no wonder people often mistook her for Allie's older sister.

Jack began setting the plates on top of the red-and-white tablecloth. "Allie hired another bartender."

Helen frowned as she set the basket at the end of the table. "What happened to that girl you hired last week?"

"It didn't work out," Allie mumbled.

She didn't miss the loaded, wordless exchange that passed between her mother and brother. Allie squeezed a napkin in her hand, wrinkling the fabric. Seemed her entire family had that look down pat. It was part pity, part worry and part helplessness. As if they wanted to save her from herself but didn't know how.

Thankfully, her parents were big on allowing their kids to make their own decisions, and not interfering with their lives. Though she suspected it about killed family members not to ask her why she'd moved back to Serenity Springs.

Especially Jack.

But she couldn't tell her brother what happened, that a lapse in judgment had led her to make a huge mistake. Or what she'd done to rectify that mistake.

The oven timer buzzed. "There's the pie," Helen said,

giving Allie's back a quick, brisk rub. She turned to leave, then sighed. "Oh, will you look at them?"

Allie followed her mom's gaze out the large picture window. "I thought you sent Dad out to get a load of firewood?"

"I did," she said, wrapping her arm around Allie's waist. "Emma insisted on helping him, and begged Kelsey to go out with them, as well."

Jack stood on Helen's other side and she linked her arm with his as they watched Larry Martin run through the knee-high snow pulling a giggling Emma on a red plastic sled. Duke, their large golden retriever, ran beside them, barking and trying to snatch Emma's hat. Kelsey, her hands stuffed into the pockets of her puffy coat, brought up the rear.

Helen shook her head and laughed softly. "I guarantee your father's going to regret that tomorrow." The oven timer was still buzzing and, after giving Allie a quick squeeze, she left.

Jack put down the last two plates. "Kelsey doesn't hold much hope this new bartender will work. Said her background was in theater and the only restaurant-bar experience she has is waiting tables."

"Actually," Allie said, placing a napkin to the left of each plate as she walked around the table, "that didn't work out, either."

Jack followed her, laying down silverware. "What do you mean?"

She acted casual as if she couldn't feel Jack's eyes were on her. "Just what I said. She found a better offer. Didn't even work a day."

"Things must've been pretty slow on a Saturday night if you got by without a bartender."

"We were swamped." She placed the last napkin and went to her mother's antique cherry sideboard for glasses. "The spring breakers hit around nine and it didn't slow until closing."

"Why didn't you call Kelsey?"

"She wasn't feeling well. Speaking of which, she seems to have recovered."

Jack followed her nod toward the window, to find Kelsey engaged in a rigorous snowball fight against Emma and Larry. Duke ran back and forth between the three, trying to catch snowballs in his mouth.

"She thinks it was something she ate." He waved his hand in dismissal. "How did you manage without a bartender?"

"I had a bartender." Allie avoided his eyes as she carried over two crystal water goblets at a time. "I hired one last night."

"What? How?"

"I hired one of my earlier applicants."

He snagged her wrist, stopping her before she could evade him again. "Tell me you didn't."

She smiled up at him and even added a few quick bats of her eyelashes for good measure. "Didn't what?"

Jack, of course, didn't buy her innocent act. "Didn't hire the cowboy."

"How did you know about him?"

He raised one eyebrow. "How do you think?"

She glared at her sister-in-law through the window.

"Your wife has a big mouth. What do you two do? Is my business pillow talk or something?"

He let go of her and crossed his arms over his chest. Sent her his most authoritative cop look. *Ha.* As if he could ever intimidate her.

"Kelsey said you didn't hire him because you didn't trust him."

"I changed my mind."

"Did you check his résumé? Follow up on his references?"

"Of course I read his résumé." She flipped her hair behind her shoulder. "I'm perfectly capable of hiring my own employees, you know."

"If you were so good at it, why have you gone through a dozen bartenders since the summer?"

"Seven. I've had seven bartenders since July." She crossed back to the sideboard for the rest of the glasses. "I'm not an idiot," she snapped. "I can handle my business."

"I realize you're not an idiot. You're one of the smartest people I know. But you also allow your emotions to get in the way of your sense sometimes." He took hold of her arms, turning her so she faced him. "You can't save the world, Allie."

Her throat constricted and she pulled away from him. "I have no interest in saving the world."

Not anymore. Not since she'd discovered that in the process, you sometimes save someone undeserving.

Too bad she hadn't remembered that before she'd saved Dean from another take-out meal by inviting him to dinner.

"You can't keep collecting strays. That kid you have working in the kitchen is a perfect example."

"So I gave Richie a break."

"He needs more than a break. He needs an intervention. Or better yet, a few months in lockup so he can detox."

"How many times do I have to tell you he's not on drugs? Not anymore."

Jack stabbed a hand through his short, dark hair. "Just because an addict tells you he's not using doesn't make it true. No matter how much you want to believe it. And what about this new guy? What's his issue? What do you even know about him?"

"I knew enough to hire him…because he was the only candidate for the job left!" she said, not caring that she sounded like a bratty, rebellious teenager.

If Jack would knock off the bossy big brother act, she wouldn't have to get so defensive.

"Desperation is no excuse. Do you know his work experience? His previous places of employment?" Jack asked. God, he was like a pit bull once he sunk his teeth into something. "I bet you didn't even check his background."

She slammed a glass down so hard she was lucky the stem didn't break off. "I know Dean can mix drinks and keep the bar running smoothly." She also knew every female in the place had been half in lust with him. And that his kiss made her want to drop-kick her self-preservation instincts off a cliff. "He can also handle difficult situations—"

"Difficult situations? Like what? Running out of lemons?"

"No," she said coldly, surprised the word didn't come out in a little burst of frost. "Things like handling a large, belligerent drunk and two of his friends who refused to leave at closing time."

A muscle jumped in Jack's jaw. "What happened?"

She waved her hand in the air. "Nothing I couldn't handle. Well, nothing Dean and I couldn't handle. Which is just the point. I'm a grown woman completely capable of taking care of myself and my business."

"If someone was giving you a hard time, you should've called me—"

"No. I shouldn't have. I don't need rescuing, Jack, and even if I did, it wouldn't be your job. Besides," she continued before he could argue, "as much as I love that you want to protect me, what I need even more from you is some trust. In me. In my decisions."

"Trust?" he asked, so harshly she winced. He glanced at the doorway to the kitchen and pulled her to the far corner, lowering his voice. "You don't want us to trust you. What you want is for us to sit on our hands and smile while you run from whatever it was that happened in New York. Whatever sent you back to Serenity Springs."

She tucked her trembling hands behind her back. "I'm not run—"

"Bullshit."

She shoved a chair into the table with enough force to rattle the glassware. "I told you when I bought The Summit why I came back. I was burned out. Disillusioned." Both of which were more true than he'd ever know. "I was working over seventy hours a week. I had no social life and no time for myself. What I did have was an endless caseload and the beginnings of an ulcer."

"You knew you'd have to work hard," Jack pointed out, bless his pragmatic heart. "All you talked about since graduating from law school was making partner at a prestigious firm before you were thirty-five."

"Sometimes what we want and what's best for us are two different things." She edged past him and went to the head of the table. Flipped the knife over so the edge faced the plate. "That's what I realized when I was offered the partnership." She slid the spoon down so the bottom of it was flush with the bottom of the knife. "It was the moment I'd worked so hard for, but when it was within my grasp, I knew it was wrong for me."

"I understand you wanted a break, that you wanted to come home," he said as he sat in the chair to her left. "I felt the same way after Nicole died. But what I don't understand is why you gave up practicing law altogether. Why buy a bar? Why not start your own practice right here?"

"I didn't like what had become of my life. What I'd become." She told him the truth. As much of it as she could admit, anyway.

"See?" Jack leaned forward. "That's what I'm talking about. What do you mean, you didn't like who you'd become?" When she remained silent he caught her hand, tugged on it until she lifted her head. "Talk to me. I want to help you."

She forced a laugh. Ignored how hollow it sounded. "I don't need any help. I'm fine. Better than fine." She pulled free of his hold. "I own my own home and my own business, which is growing and thriving. Deciding to step away from practicing law wasn't an easy decision—actually, it was one of the hardest decisions I've ever had to make—but I made the right choice. All I need now is for the people I love to believe that as well."

She held her breath as he took in what she'd said. "I do believe you coming home was for the best," he said. "Never doubt that."

She exhaled softly. *Thank God.* Maybe this time she'd finally gotten through to him. Her big brother was nothing if not incredibly stubborn.

"What I don't believe," he said, "are any of the reasons you gave me for why you came home. But I'm willing to let it drop. For now. When you're ready to tell me the whole truth, I'll be waiting."

She kept her shoulders back and pressed a hand against her churning stomach. As soon as Jack left the room, she slumped into a chair, but the nausea remained. How could she tell him what had really happened? What she'd done, why she'd returned to Serenity Springs? If he knew, he'd try to stop her.

She still had so much more to make up for. People who depended on her to keep their secrets. To keep them safe.

And most importantly, to keep them hidden.

AT TEN TO SIX, Dean stepped up onto the Martins' porch. He shifted the bouquet of flowers from his right hand to his left and knocked on the door. A few moments later, it opened to reveal a tall, dark-haired man.

Dean had thoroughly researched everything there was to know about Allison Martin. Including the glowering man before him. Jack Martin. Serenity Springs's chief of police. Ex-NYPD detective. And Allison's older brother.

Dean took in Martin's dark expression, the suspicion in his eyes. It wasn't going to be so easy to fool the good chief here.

Dean loved a challenge.

"Something I can do for you?" Martin asked, his body blocking the doorway.

"I'm Dean Garret," he said, keeping his free hand loose at his side. He didn't doubt Martin would rather slap cuffs on his wrists sooner than shake his hand. "Allison invited me to dinner."

"She did, did she?" he asked in a low, dangerous tone.

"Your skills are slipping," Allie said to her brother as she sauntered up behind him. "After all, you helped set the table. Didn't you notice the extra place setting?"

"Guess I was too busy trying to figure out what in the hell you were doing with your life."

And Dean couldn't help but wonder what Jack meant. Did he have his own suspicions about his sister?

Allie nudged Jack with her hip, then brushed past him. She gestured to Dean. "Come on in."

He took off his hat and stepped into the narrow foyer as she shut the door. He could hear the faint sounds of voices and smell roast beef and a wood fire. After his parents' divorce, his mother couldn't afford the upkeep on the house, so they'd moved onto the ranch Dean's grandparents owned. His mother's favorite part about returning to her childhood home was having a fireplace again. During the holidays, she'd always insisted they light a fire even though there was rarely a need for one. She'd said it created ambience.

"Those are so beautiful," Allie said, taking the flowers from him. She pressed her nose against them and inhaled. "Thank you."

"They're not for you. They're for your mother."

"You are one smart man. She's going to love them. Here, let me take your coat."

Dean shrugged out of it as Jack cleared his throat.

"Oh, right. Dean," Allie said as she jerked a thumb behind her, "this is my overprotective, overbearing, slightly anal brother, Jack."

Jack didn't so much as blink. "Actually, it's Police Chief Jack Martin."

"For the love of God," Allie muttered. "Yes, my brother is not only very scary with that glower he's got going on, but he's also really intimidating. And since you now know he's the—" she held up the flowers and made quotation marks in the air "—chief of police, I'm sure we can trust you not to steal the silverware."

"And I was hoping to add another spoon to my collection," Dean said.

Allie pursed her lips. "I thought you collected panties?"

"Do I even want to know how you'd know that?" Jack asked.

She patted his chest. "Probably not."

"I should've traded you for Melinda Hatchett's puppy when you were three, but Mom and Dad wouldn't let me," the chief said in an easy tone that didn't hide his frustration.

"Oh, ha ha." Allie cuffed his arm. "I'll remember that

this Mother's Day when you come crying to me to help you pick out the perfect gift. And this year you have two mothers to buy for."

Jack winced. "Have I ever told you you're my favorite sister?"

"It's too late to suck up now." But Dean noticed she squeezed Jack's arm. "Of course, bribes are always welcome. And don't think Rachel didn't tell me you said *she* was your favorite at the wedding."

Rachel, Dean knew, was the youngest Martin sibling, a doctor who lived in New York City. Dean stood there, hat in hand, and watched the byplay between this brother and sister. He hadn't been sure what to expect. With Jack being a cop and Allie a defense attorney, he'd wondered if there would be friction between her and her family.

He had his answer.

But were they so close that Jack would do anything for her? Would he break the law? Bend it a little and use his love for his sister as justification? Would he help hide a woman and child?

Dean couldn't fault Allie for helping Lynne Addison keep her son away from a possible pedophile. Even if he did wonder how she could represent the man in court in the first place. But when Lynne took Jon with no custodial agreement, she'd broken the law.

The same law Jack Martin had taken an oath to uphold.

Allie tossed Dean's coat at Jack and then gestured for Dean to follow her. He made a mental note to dig into the police chief's past. There was right and there was wrong. And wearing a uniform and a badge didn't absolve a man from those two basic facts. Facts that Dean based his career on. Based his life on.

He followed Allie into the kitchen. The room was a mixture of dark and light—cream walls, white cabinets, granite countertops and a rich, wide-board cherrywood floor.

"Dean, these are my parents, Larry and Helen Martin," Allie said. "Mom, Dad, this is Dean Garret. My new bartender."

"Nice to meet you, sir," Dean said, shaking Mr. Martin's hand. He knew Larry Martin had also been a cop, retiring a few years back from the position his son now held. Allie's dad was a few inches shorter than his son, with more gray than black in his short hair. Dean turned to Allie's mother. "I appreciate you having me for dinner."

"You're more than welcome," Mrs. Martin said.

"We're used to Allie bringing home strays," Jack said drily.

"Shut it," Allie told her brother in a singsong voice. "Dean brought you these flowers, Mom."

"How lovely." She took the bouquet and smiled as she trailed her fingertips over the petals. "Thank you, Dean."

He nodded, feeling an odd, fluttering sensation in his stomach. If he didn't know better, he would've sworn it was guilt trying to worm its way past his defenses. Which was nuts. He didn't feel guilty about working this case.

Of course, he'd never been invited to share Sunday dinner with someone he was investigating.

"You've met Kelsey," Allie said.

"Nice to see you again," he told the redhead.

Kelsey smirked at Allie, then wiggled her eyebrows. Allie coughed as if covering a laugh. "And this," she continued quickly as a little girl scampered into the room, her dark blond hair in two high pigtails on top of her head, "is my niece, Emma."

Dean liked kids. Really. But they never failed to remind him of what he'd lost. Even his former partner's three children. If he was still on speaking terms with his family, he'd have more experience around kids, since his brother Ryan and his new wife had a one-year-old daughter. A niece Dean had never met.

If only Ryan's new wife hadn't, at one time, been Dean's old wife.

If only Ryan didn't have what Dean had thought he'd never wanted—and would probably never have.

He crouched so he and Emma were eye to eye. "Nice to meet you."

She pressed her small, warm hand into his. He gently closed his fingers around it, hyperaware of her delicate bones.

Allie playfully tugged one of Emma's pigtails. "Aren't you going to say hello?"

The child's grin widened, revealing a missing tooth on the bottom. She waved.

Allie laughed. "What's gotten into you? Cat got your tongue?"

Emma shook her head so hard her hair almost hit Dean in the face. He straightened. When she stopped shaking like a wet dog, she stuck her tongue out at Allie.

"Emma…" Jack said sternly.

"Relax," Kelsey said, moving to stand next to him.

He slid his arm around her waist. "She's showing Allie that she still has her tongue."

Emma nodded.

Helen walked by, carrying a bowl of mashed potatoes. "She hasn't said a word since she came inside."

"That's because she's not talking," Kelsey said. "At least not until dessert. Right, Emma?"

Again, the blonde pixie nodded. She sure was a cute little thing.

Allie picked up the bowl of rolls; from the slight rise of steam Dean figured they were still warm. "I thought it was physically impossible for Emma not to speak. What's going on?" she asked.

"You'll see," Kelsey said with a sly grin.

"Ooh…a secret, huh?" Allie handed the rolls to Jack. "I bet some tickling could get her to spill the beans."

This obviously wasn't the first time Allie and her niece had played this game. No sooner had Allie said the word *tickling* than Emma gave a high-pitched shriek and bolted, Allie hot on her heels. Larry lifted the platter of sliced roast and sidestepped the pair as they raced out of the kitchen.

"Everyone take your seat," Helen said. She opened a drawer and pulled out a corkscrew. "Jack, please tell your sister to stop chasing Emma so we can all sit down."

The pair in question burst back into the kitchen, Emma still giggling. Before Dean could evade her, she clutched his leg and swung herself around behind him.

Allie skid to a stop. "No fair."

Emma giggled again.

"Come on, squirt," Jack said, picking up his daughter. "The sooner we eat dinner, the sooner we'll get dessert."

At the table, Dean held out Allie's chair for her, ignoring the chief's scowl. He took his own seat and forced his mind to clear. To stop thinking about how all of this—the house, the food, the closeness of these people—reminded him of his own family.

Of how they used to be.

And he couldn't believe he was going to admit this, even to himself, but he really did feel guilty, after all. That guilt made him even more uncomfortable when Larry Martin said grace and everyone bowed their heads.

So what if they'd welcomed Dean into their home? Allowed him to share a meal with them? He had to keep his focus. Just because the Martins seemed like a nice family—hell, they probably *were* a nice family—that didn't make a difference to him or what he had to do.

Without lifting his head, he glanced over to find Jack watching him, mistrust clear in his cold gaze. Dean also had to remember he wasn't dealing with regular civilians here. Not that some small town chief of police worried Dean. By the time Jack figured out what he was really doing in Serenity Springs—*if* he figured it out— Dean would be long gone.

And he'd have the one thing he'd come here to collect.

A missing woman and her child.

CHAPTER SIX

DINNER PASSED WITHOUT incident. Thank God. But Allie wasn't taking any chances. She turned on the coffeepot and took down the good cups and saucers from the upper cabinet. During a delicious meal of tender roast beef and all the trimmings, the conversation had been steered toward neutral subjects.

Mainly because Allie had rarely allowed Jack or her father to get a word in edgewise.

Or to ask Dean too many personal questions.

Sure, she was curious about Dean herself, but wanted him to open up on his own. Not because he was being interrogated.

After Allie convinced her mom she deserved to relax after doing most of the cooking, Helen, along with her husband, Kelsey and Emma, went into the living room. Jack and Dean stayed behind to help Allie clear the table.

Her best bet would be to keep her brother and Dean as far away from each other as possible. Easier said than done, since Jack seemed more interested in loading the dishwasher than joining his wife and daughter in the other room.

Dean came into the kitchen and set a stack of dirty plates on the counter. "Anything I can do to help?"

"You wash," she said, tossing a towel over her shoulder before handing him a bottle of liquid soap, "and I'll dry."

He unbuttoned his sleeves at the wrist and rolled them to his elbows before squirting in soap and filling the sink with hot water.

"We've got this under control," she told Jack, who'd just added detergent to the dishwasher. "Why don't you join everyone else?"

"No sense you two doing all the work." He snatched the towel off her shoulder. "Besides, this is a great opportunity for me to get to know your new employee."

Oh, she didn't like that glint in her brother's eyes.

"Allie says you're new in town," Jack said to Dean. He held the towel out of Allie's reach when she tried to grab it.

"I got in on Wednesday."

"What made you come to Serenity Springs?"

Dean washed and rinsed the gravy boat. Handed it to Jack. "I heard about the job opening. Thought I'd check it out."

"Not very many people outside of town have heard about The Summit." Jack handed the dry dish to Allie to put away. "Or that it had an opening for a bartender."

"That was so subtle," Allie said. "Don't tell me, when you were in New York, you always got to play the bad cop?"

"Only on even days." He dried a bowl. "I'm trying

to get to know our guest. Unless—" he glanced at Dean "—you have something to hide?"

"He doesn't." She snatched the bowl from him. "But that doesn't mean you have the right to interrogate him, either."

"I spent the last few months in Syracuse," Dean said mildly, "and I saw the ad for the job opening online."

"Syracuse?" Jack asked. "That's a long way from... where is it you said you were from? Denver?"

Dean kept his head down as he scrubbed the roasting pan. Why were men who were up to their elbows in dish suds so damn sexy? "Dallas."

"How'd you end up in Syracuse?"

Allie managed to snatch the towel out of Jack's hands. She stood between the men and glared at her brother, her hands fisted on her hips. "What is up with the interrogation?"

She'd hate for Dean to be scared away by Jack's tough cop routine. Plus, it was humiliating to have Jack acting like they were teenagers again and she'd brought home a boy for the first time.

"It's all right." Dean skimmed his wet fingers over her arm, giving her goose bumps. "A buddy of mine from the Corps lives in Syracuse. He got me a job at a hotel his sister managed there."

"Since you're here, I take it that didn't work out. Did you get fired?"

She squeezed the towel between her hands and pretended it was her brother's fat neck. "Jack, I swear—"

"My full name is Dean William Garret," he said, shifting so that he stood beside her, facing Jack. Though his voice was still low, she detected a thread of impatience. "Allison has my social security number and birth date from my job application. I was born and raised outside of Dallas, joined up when I was twenty-one and spent the next nine years in the service."

"You don't have to tell him any of this," Allie said.

Dean dried his hands on the towel she still held. "As you said, I have nothing to hide."

She bit her lower lip. She believed that. Didn't she?

"I'm divorced," he continued. "No kids. I served in both Afghanistan and Iraq. After my discharge—"

"Honorable?" Jack asked.

Allie tossed the towel at him, but he caught it before it hit his face. "You are going to pay for this," she promised.

Jack slung the towel around his neck, held on to the ends. "You'll thank me if he's AWOL and they have a warrant out for him."

This whole thing was surreal. Jack had always been overprotective, but he was going overboard. Just because she'd been taken advantage of by a few of her previous employees… It was as if she was seeing her brother as a cop, for the first time.

She couldn't say she much cared for it.

And honestly, witnessing these two facing off was getting on her nerves. Jack was cool and in control, while Dean stood unflinching, his attitude laid-back. But his body was tense, as if gearing up for a fight.

And wouldn't that be a lovely way to end the evening?

"I'm not AWOL," Dean said. "I served my country and was honorably discharged."

"And haven't had a steady job since?" Jack pressed.

"That's it," Allie snapped as she seized Jack's arm and hauled him toward the door. "Go into the living room and cool your jets," she told him "and maybe I'll speak to you again in five years."

"I was trying—"

"Yeah, yeah. You were trying to help. Trying to protect me. I get it." She shook her head, unable to keep the anger and disappointment out of her voice as she said, "But you overstepped, Jack."

He stared at Dean for two long heartbeats before nodding.

Her shoulders slumped as she watched Jack disappear into the living room.

"You all right?" Dean asked.

She straightened and faced him. "Fine." She crossed back to the counter and picked up a large serving tray. Yanking open the silverware drawer, she scooped up a handful of dessert forks. "I'd apologize for my brother, but really, what's the point?"

Dean let the water out of the sink. "He's just doing his job."

She slammed the drawer shut. "Even cops have days off."

"Not that job." He dried his hands. "The job of watching out for you. That's what older brothers are for."

"Is that what you do for your brothers?"

His hesitation was brief but noticeable. "I think it's different with sisters."

She tossed the forks onto the tray with a loud clang. "Why do you do that?"

"Do what?"

"Give me a nonanswer when I ask you something? If it's too personal, just say so."

"It's too personal."

"See?" she asked irritably. "That wasn't so hard." She turned her back on him, set dessert plates on the tray before spinning around again. "It's not like I expect you to share all your secrets with me just because I hired you—despite your less than stellar résumé."

His brow furrowed. "You hired me because you were desperate."

She waved that distinction away. "I'm giving you a chance."

"And I appreciate it."

"I don't want your gratitude," she almost growled.

"What do you want then?"

A straight answer. To stop feeling like she'd been wrong to hire him. To trust him.

She wanted him to do or say something that would put her mind at ease about him.

"Nothing." She went to the refrigerator for the milk. "I'm sorry. I'm mad at Jack and taking it out on you." She poured milk into a ceramic creamer. "It's not like we're friends, right? And it's obvious you want to keep it that way—"

"You're my boss," he pointed out.

She flashed him a forced smile as she put the milk away, opened the freezer and took out a gallon of vanilla ice cream. She set it on the counter. "That I am. And even though I have friendships with several of my employees—and am related to my manager—you and

I will keep our relationship strictly business from here on out."

Despite the fact that she'd invited him to Sunday dinner. And that he'd accepted.

Or that he'd kissed her last night.

He shoved a hand through his hair. "I doubt someone like you needs any more friends. You probably have more than you know what to do with."

"True." She put the coffeepot on the tray along with the sugar bowl. "I just thought…"

"What?"

"I thought maybe you could use one."

He looked shocked and, to her surprise, insulted. "I'm an island."

She grinned. "Like I said, I'll leave you alone. Can you get the tray for me, please?"

She picked up the apple pie and ice cream and headed to the door. She'd made it to the threshold when he said, "It's nothing personal."

"You don't have to ex—"

"I had a…falling out with my family," he said, unrolling his sleeves, "and we haven't spoken for a while."

"I'm sorry." Even as mad as she was with Jack, she couldn't imagine not seeing him, talking with him—or anyone else in her family. "I shouldn't have pressed. Let's forget I said anything."

"I hate spiders."

She frowned. Maybe all of this talk about opening up had pushed the poor guy over the edge. "Excuse me?"

"Spiders." He shoved his hands into his pockets. "I hate them."

She adjusted her grip so that the pie pressed against her rib cage, taking some of the weight off her wrist. Dean seemed at ease in her mother's kitchen. He leaned back against the counter, his shoulders relaxed, his long legs stretched out in front of him.

But there was a challenge in his eyes. As if he was daring her to say something about what he'd admitted. And that's when she realized he didn't just hate spiders. He was afraid of them.

He'd shared one of his secrets with her.

"I won't tell a soul," she promised, shifting the ice cream so she could make an X across her heart.

"I appreciate that." But despite the slight upward curve of his mouth, he didn't really seem amused. If anything, he seemed…triumphant. Almost predatory. She could only stare as he closed the distance between them. "What about you?" he asked, reaching out as if to touch her cheek. But then he fisted his hand and dropped his arm back to his side. "Any secrets you'd like to share?"

She swallowed in an attempt to work moisture back into her mouth. "Nothing quite as dark as arachnophobia."

"You sure?" His eyes were steady. Intense. "Because you know what they say about confession being good for the soul."

Except she didn't need confession. Not when she'd already taken care of her penance on her own.

"I'm positive."

"Everyone has secrets, Allison. And I'm guessing yours are more interesting than most." He leaned forward and she slanted back, kept the ice cream and pie between them. "Guess I have my work cut out for me," he murmured.

Fear, irrational and unsettling, filled her. "What work is that?"

One side of his mouth lifted. "Finding out what your secrets are."

ALLISON'S FACE DRAINED OF color and she took a hasty step back. "I…they're waiting for us…."

Then she raced out of the room.

Dean scratched the side of his neck. *Smooth move, Garret. Scare the hell out of her. Good plan. That'll make it easier to find out where Lynne and Jon are.*

He made it to the hallway before remembering the tray in the kitchen. With a mild curse, he headed back the way he'd come.

He could do this. He'd fought in the mountains of Afghanistan and the streets of Baghdad. All he had to do was get through coffee and dessert, make more inane small talk. Ignore Chief Martin's suspicious glare and leading questions.

Dean would rather be on a recon mission searching for suspected terrorists.

He picked up the tray and walked out of the kitchen. He'd accepted Allie's dinner invitation so he'd be able to subtly pump her family for information about her. Or better yet, get her to open up—or in this case, slip up—and give him a clue he was searching in the right direction.

He hadn't counted on her brother being as anxious for information about him as he was about Allie.

Dean went into the living room. A sofa faced two plump armchairs in front of the fireplace, a glass-topped coffee table between them. Kelsey sat in one chair, Emma wiggling—either in excitement or because she had to go to the bathroom—on her lap. Jack sat at his wife's feet.

Helen and Larry were on the sofa. Dean raised his eyebrows when he noted their linked hands. Maybe Nolan and Cassie weren't the only happily married couple in the world.

Just one of the few.

Allie, perched on the second armchair, didn't so much as glance up when he entered the room.

"Thank you, Dean," Helen said as she rose. "You can set it on the coffee table."

"Great. As soon as everyone has their dessert, Emma can share her secret," Kelsey said. "She's had enough of being silent. Poor kid's about to bust."

Allie slid a slice of pie onto a plate, then handed it to Jack, who added a scoop of ice cream. "I think it's cruel you made her stay silent for so long."

Kelsey set Emma down and accepted the plate from Jack. "Hey, it was her idea. She wanted to make a big production out of this secret, not me. And she thought the safest way not to spill the beans early was if she didn't speak at all."

"Dean, please sit down," Helen said, indicating the end of the sofa across from Allie. "Coffee?"

He nodded and sat as Helen served it and Allie dished up the pie. He accepted his piece and took a bite, almost groaning in pleasure. Sweet, warm apple filling wrapped in a crust as flaky as his mother's. What could be better? He refused to feel ashamed about accepting their hospitality—and their damned good pie—under false pretenses. And while he knew better than to like the people he was investigating, it was easy to like the Martins.

He flicked a glance at Jack. Well, most of the Martins.

But liking them was okay. As long as it didn't interfere with the job.

Reaching for a napkin, Allie leaned forward, giving Dean a peek at her cleavage and the lacy edge of her cream-colored bra. He choked on a mouthful of cinnamon-laced apples.

And found Jack staring at him.

"You all right?" Allie asked, her elbows on her knees.

She was torturing him. He stole another look at Jack. Or else she was trying to get him killed.

"I'm fine," he wheezed. He took a large sip of his coffee and cleared his throat. "Sorry."

"Well, kiddo, it's time," Kelsey said, pulling a piece of glossy white paper out of her back pocket. She handed it to Emma, who pressed it against her chest. "You ready to share your news?"

The child skipped to the center of the room, her grin huge and excited. "Look," Emma ordered, shoving the paper in Allie's face.

Allie leaned back as if to better focus on the picture, then her expression softened. "Oh…" she breathed in that awed tone women used when they came across puppies, babies or a man who brought them flowers for no reason "…it's an ultrasound."

Larry leaped up with a whoop, practically hurdled the table and enfolded Jack in a bear hug. Helen, a bit slower to her feet but just as enthusiastic, hurried over to Kelsey, tears in her eyes as she hugged her daughter-in-law. Allie picked up Emma and joined her mother and sister-in-law in one of those group hugs women liked.

Everyone started talking at once. Questions and answers about due dates and morning sickness, baby names and cravings flew around the room. Jack clarified it was too early to tell if the baby was a boy or girl, but Emma, obviously hoping for that brother, told him in no uncertain terms it was a boy. She was sure of it. Allie asked if Kelsey wanted to cut back her hours. Helen talked about getting the old crib out of the attic, and Larry went to get a bottle of wine—and ginger ale for Kelsey and Emma—so they could share a toast.

And Dean sat there, his blood cold as he took it all in.

His hands were unsteady as he set his cup and plate on the table. He'd been here before. Except the last time he'd been to a family function where someone announced a pregnancy, it'd been his brother Ryan announcing the woman he loved was pregnant with his child.

And then Dean had lost control and broken Ryan's nose.

He forced himself to get to his feet and calmly walk over to Allie.

She was now hugging Jack, so Dean waited until she'd let go of her brother before touching her elbow. "I'm going to head out."

She was so happy, it was almost painful to witness. "What? But why?"

"This should be a private celebration," he said. He

then thanked Helen for her hospitality and congratulated Kelsey and Jack.

"Let me get your coat," Allie said, following him out into the hallway.

Larry came down the hall carrying wineglasses by their stems in one hand, a bottle of wine in the other. "Allie, can you get the ginger ale?"

"Sure, Dad. I'm going to walk Dean out first."

"I appreciate you having me in your home," Dean said.

"You're more than welcome, son," Larry said. "We're always happy to meet Allie's friends."

Sweet God but some people were gullible. Thankfully, Dean wasn't the type of man to succumb to guilt.

Allie opened the closet door and reached up to the shelf for his hat. "Damn you, Jack," she muttered, her fingers barely grazing the brim.

His Stetson was at the back of the shelf—right where Chief Martin must've tossed it. Dean also noticed Allie's jacket, the red leather one she'd worn the other day, hanging to the left.

"Let me help you," Dean said, coming up behind her.

He reached for the hat, trapping her between the coats and his body. His arm brushed her shoulder and she twitched. With his fingers curled around the brim of his hat, he stepped back out into the hall.

Where he could breathe.

She handed him his coat without meeting his eyes. Laughter broke out in the other room and she glanced over her shoulder.

"I can see myself out," he said.

"Are you sure?"

He nodded, kept his expression blank. "I'd hate for you to miss any of the celebration. Go back to your family." He put his hat on. "I'll see you Tuesday."

She looked at the front door and, obviously feeling he'd be able to handle leaving on his own, said, "Okay, then. Good night, Dean."

Instead of watching the sway of her hips as she walked down the hall, he stared into the closet at Allie's red leather jacket. Shrugged his coat on as he remembered her putting her cell phone in her pocket last night.

After making sure the hallway was empty, he wrapped a scarf around his hand, reached into Allie's right coat pocket and picked up her phone. He then dropped it into his own pocket and put the scarf back.

He kept his strides unhurried as he left the house. Standing under the porch light, he buttoned his coat. Despite the cold, the sky was clear and there were almost as many stars visible as there were back home.

Best of all, his evening hadn't been a total waste.

He patted the pocket with Allie's phone as he made his way down the steps. The snow beneath his feet crunched and the cold air stung his lungs. He couldn't wait to get back to Texas.

He'd discovered a few useful things tonight. Such as there was no sense trying to gain information about Allie from her family. The way Chief Martin had acted, Dean knew it would be in his best interest to keep as low a profile as possible during his remaining time in town.

He unlocked his truck, slid inside and started the engine before he even shut the door. He'd also learned that Allie truly was one of those people who lived to help others, which played into his theory that she'd helped the Addisons run away from a pedophile.

And though Dean had taken a misstep in the kitchen by admitting he wanted to discover her secrets, Allie's reaction had confirmed what he'd already suspected.

She was hiding something.

He pulled away from the curb and turned the radio up when Brad Paisley's latest came on.

But he still couldn't figure out why Allie had represented Miles Addison in the first place. Of course, even Lynne's mother had admitted to being tricked into believing Miles was innocent. Maybe Allie had been, too?

Not that it mattered; he didn't need to figure out Allison Martin and her motives. All he needed to do was find Lynne and Jon. Whether they wanted to be reunited with Robin—or even wanted to be found—wasn't his concern.

All he cared about was completing this job.

And moving on to the next one.

"HEY, RICHIE," Allie said late Monday morning as she walked into The Summit's kitchen.

She was running late after spending almost an hour with her cell phone provider, reporting her lost phone. She'd discovered it missing last night when she got home. When her mom couldn't find it either, Allie had canceled her service.

Only to find her phone wedged in back of the driver's seat not twenty minutes later. She'd missed it last night—which was what she got for searching her car in the dark—and would've missed it today if she hadn't spilled the large coffee she'd bought at Sweet Suggestions.

She really hated Mondays.

She unwound the scarf from her neck and narrowed her eyes at her assistant—or, as he liked to think of himself, her sous-chef. Richie's brown hair was covered with a baseball cap, his stubby ponytail pulled through the hole in the back, his thin face was pale, his brown eyes watery.

"You feeling all right?" she asked him.

"Yeah, I'm good." He stopped chopping onions long enough to take a long drink from his water bottle. "I think I'm coming down with a cold, that's all."

"You sure you're up for working today?" She slipped off her coat and laid it over the back of a chair before going to him at the counter. "You know how slow Mondays are. I'm sure I could manage without you."

"I'll be okay."

"If you say so. But let me know if you feel worse. I talked to Ellen earlier and both she and Bobby have head colds, so it's definitely going around." Ellen Jensen, Allie's hairdresser, had called to change Allie's appointment to Wednesday, hoping her son would be back in school by then.

Allie dug a notepad and pen out of a drawer. "Why don't I make tortilla soup tonight? Sort of my Mexican version of chicken noodle soup, minus the noodles." She wrote a list of the ingredients she'd need. "Can you run to the store for me? And it'd be better if I handled the food prep tonight. We don't want any contamination."

Richie took the list, shoved it into the pocket of his baggy jeans. "It's not like I spit in the food," he muttered. "I wash my hands after using the bathroom and everything."

She raised her eyebrows at his tone. "You sure you're all right?"

He dropped his eyes and shrugged his bony shoulders, looking more like a teenager than a man of twenty-three. "Sorry. Guess I'm not feeling as well as I thought."

"Why don't you forget the groceries? I'm sure I'll have time later—"

"Nah. I've got it." He took his coat from one of the hooks on the wall. "I'll get the groceries, drop them off and then maybe head home for a quick nap. Some sleep will make me feel better. Besides, I don't want to leave you hanging. Mondays might not be the busiest but they're usually pretty steady."

Wasn't he sweet? She'd definitely made the right decision to hire him, no matter what Jack said. Yes, Richie had previously had a problem with drugs, but he did his best each day to fight it. To make a better life for himself.

And she was helping him do it.

"All right," Allie said, taking her wallet out of her purse. She handed him a fifty and a couple of twenties. "If the avocados are decent, get a few extra and I'll make guacamole, too. And you'd better see if Kelsey needs anything for the bar."

He put on his coat and pocketed the money before pulling on his knit hat and picking up his water bottle. "I should be back in a couple of hours," he said, then pushed through the door to the dining room.

Allie washed her hands and finished chopping onions. Scooping them into a large bowl, she covered it and stuck it in the refrigerator.

"Can you call Noreen for me?" she asked Kelsey, who was mopping the floor in the barroom. "See if she can come in and help me prep dinner?"

"Hello. I'm great, thanks for asking." Kelsey stuck the mop into the industrial bucket. "Second day in a row I haven't thrown up my breakfast. Although I almost did when I walked into the kitchen and smelled those onions Richie was cutting."

Allie wrinkled her nose and went behind the bar. "I think I liked our relationship better when you didn't share quite so much information."

"Just doing my best to keep you abreast of all of this pregnancy stuff. You know, so you're not shocked when it happens to you."

Allie clenched her hands, her fingernails digging into her palms. It'd been a long time since she'd considered a family of her own. "I don't think we have to worry about that happening anytime soon, seeing as I haven't even been on a date in more than five months."

Kelsey dunked the mop in the soapy water a few times and then set it in the wringer. "You brought a guy to Sunday dinner at your parents' house."

"That wasn't a date. I felt bad for Dean being alone in town."

Kelsey mopped under a table. "Uh-huh."

"I did," she insisted, stopping shy of adding a foot stomp for good measure. She filled a glass with ice and took a bottle of cranberry juice from the minifridge. "And I honestly don't see why Jack had to be so overprotective. I've invited both Richie and Noreen for dinner before, too."

"Yeah, but to my knowledge, neither Richie nor Noreen ever stared at you as if you were a Dallas Cowboy-cheerleader—complete with hot pants."

Allie poured juice into her glass and shook her head. "Where do you come up with this stuff?"

"Hey, I'm calling it like I see it, that's all." Finished mopping, she took a chair off the table and set it down. "Although Dillon often asks me that same question."

"It doesn't matter." Allie added lemon-lime soda to her juice and gave it a quick stir with a straw. "Even if Dean did look at me in that way, I'm not going there."

She sipped her drink. Their kiss the other night had been an acknowledgment of the attraction between them. A way of diffusing that attraction, and the curiosity that went along with it, before it became an issue.

One they'd have to act on.

But she couldn't chance a relationship with someone she didn't trust completely. She couldn't risk getting too close to anyone and having her secret come out.

"I'm glad to hear it," Kelsey said, dragging the bucket toward the pool table.

"That's a switch. Usually you're telling me to loosen up." She put the juice back and shut the door with her foot before coming to stand on the other side of the bar. "Last month you thought I should hook up with that ski instructor."

"I wasn't trying to pimp you out. I thought you could have fun with the guy. Enjoy life a bit."

"Hey, I do enjoy life."

"You don't have a life," Kelsey said, sitting on a stool next to Allie. "You spend most of your time here, and the only people you hang out with are your family, Dillon and Nina, and once in a while Ellen and her kid."

"I like being here," Allie muttered. "And so what if I hang out with my family and a few close friends? I love you all."

"God." Kelsey's eyes welled with tears. "No fair getting sappy around the pregnant lady." She pressed the heels of her hands against her eyes. "Stupid hormones."

Allie patted Kelsey's knee. "Aww…you're nothing but a big softie."

"Be that as it may, I do love you," Kelsey said, surprising Allie by squeezing her hand. "You're the best friend I've ever had."

"Now you're going to get me started," Allie complained, blinking furiously. "Are hormonal fluctuations catching?"

"No, and you can't use my pregnancy as an excuse for your weepiness, so suck it up and focus." Her mouth thinned. "I'm not so sure hiring Dean was the best idea."

"Weren't you the one who wanted me to hire him to begin with?"

"Hey, I'm allowed to change my mind. Which I did after witnessing you two last night. But, since you hired him, I think you should be careful. When a man looks at a woman like Dean Garret looks at you, he wants something. Something more than getting you into bed."

Allie twirled her straw between her fingers. "I think Jack is rubbing off on you. And not in a good way."

What else could she say? That she'd had the same concerns about Dean last night when he'd made that comment about discovering her secrets? About having his work cut out for him? Why should both of them worry she'd messed up?

Besides, she'd already decided to watch herself around Dean. Maybe his comment had been harmless. After all, she'd started that conversation as a way to get him to open up, to somehow forge a friendship between them. Maybe that had been his way of responding in kind.

But in case it wasn't, Allie would be sure to keep her guard up around him, and keep her secrets to herself.

CHAPTER SEVEN

"WE HAVE A PROBLEM," Dean said at work Wednesday night as Allie walked by him on her way to clear tables.

She brushed her hair from her face. "If it's another drunk who's being unreasonable, you are not to punch him. Not under any circumstances."

He motioned for her to follow him to the back of the bar, where they could talk in private and he could still keep an eye on everything. Tonight was even slower than Tuesday had been—which was saying something—but there were two couples who'd stuck around after dinner, and a group of college kids playing darts.

Of course, it wasn't even eleven. Still early. And on Tuesday, they'd had a decent-sized crowd by midnight.

"I don't go around punching every drunk who annoys me," he said. What did she think he was? Some newbie recruit on his first mission? "Just the ones who deserve it."

"There's nothing I like more than a man with his own warped code of honor," she said drily. "So, what's this problem we have?"

"I guess I shouldn't have said *we*," he clarified, curling his fingers into his palm. "More like you have a problem. Or at least, that guy you have doing dishes has a problem."

One of the college kids came up to the bar and Dean went to take his order, gesturing for Allie to follow. After getting the student a beer, he rang up the order on the cash register.

"Your assistant's using," he told her quietly.

"Who? Richie?" She looked over her shoulder. "That's ridiculous. He's been clean for more than nine months now."

Dean raised his eyebrows. So she knew the guy was an addict, but had hired him anyway?

"Then he's using again. Have you seen him today? He's on something."

Her hand shook as she picked up the rag and wiped the bar. "He's sick," she insisted, "not stoned. He's probably just loopy from the cold meds he's taking."

Was she for real? While Dean appreciated her trusting nature—it made his own job that much easier—he sure didn't like the idea of anyone else taking advantage of her.

He shoved his sleeves up and washed a glass, scrubbing harder than necessary. Not that he was taking advantage of her. He was doing his job. He wasn't using her. And after he found out for sure whether or not she knew where Lynne and Jon were, he'd be on his way.

But it wouldn't affect Allie. She wouldn't get hurt.

That Richie guy was another story.

She was watching Dean expectantly, as if waiting for him to agree with her. "I'm sure his pupils are dilated because of his cold," he said sarcastically. "And he's probably picking at his arms because of his medicine's side effects."

"You're wrong." She seized hold of the bottle of

spray disinfectant and, even though they had three hours until closing, squirted cleaner. "I know Richie." She vigorously wiped the bar. "You don't."

"True." Dean stepped back when she started spraying again, saving himself from asphyxiation by taking the bottle out of her hand. "But just to be certain, when you go back in the kitchen, why don't you take a good look at him? His hands are trembling and he can't meet anyone's eyes."

"Maybe you intimidate him."

"Me?" Dean laid his free hand on his chest. "Darlin', I'm harmless."

"That's not quite the word I'd use to describe you."

"Check it out. The guy's got all the signs."

The glare she sent him told him she wasn't too happy with his pressuring her about this. Or about the possibility of him being right.

Good thing he didn't care if she was happy with him or not.

"I'm not going to accuse a trusted employee—and someone I consider a friend—of doing drugs," she said coldly. "Especially when I don't have proof. And I'd appreciate it if, in the future, you keep your baseless accusations to yourself."

He ground his teeth together to keep from blasting her. She didn't want his help? Fine. He had better things to do.

"Yes, ma'am." He handed her the cleaner. "I'll be sure to mind my own business from here on out."

With all the disdain and superiority of a queen to a peasant, she snatched the bottle from him and stalked off.

Guess she hadn't liked his conciliatory tone.

A woman who'd entered the bar while he and Allie were talking requested a glass of white wine. Dean filled the order and fought his growing irritation. So what if Allie had an addict working for her. She was an intelligent and capable woman. Sooner or later she'd figure out that she needed to get rid of Richie.

If she didn't, Dean was sure her brother would protect her.

He glanced over to where Allie was wiping off a table. Today she had on a deep green top, snug dark jeans and black heels. The college kids were having a great time checking out her ass. But she either didn't know she was fueling their fantasies or didn't care.

More than likely she was too ticked off at him to notice.

Not that she had any reason to be angry. He'd only been trying to help. It'd taken him two days to say anything about his suspicions in the first place.

After his slipup Sunday at her parents' house, he'd taken a step back. Hadn't wanted to give Allie any reason to think he was more than what he seemed. Especially after he'd taken her cell phone, noted all outgoing and incoming calls, and gotten enough information for Nolan to hack into her personal account. Dean had then slipped over to her house late that night, broken into her vehicle and planted the phone where it would look as if she'd dropped it.

The way this case was going, though, he shouldn't worry about having his true motives revealed. He wasn't any closer to proving Allie knew where Lynn and Jon were hiding. Maybe he should just confront her.

Nolan had discovered two phone numbers Allie had called frequently over the past year. Both were to cell phones and when he and Dean had learned the first belonged to a Sheila Garey in Salem, Oregon, they thought they'd caught their first real break.

Sheila, it turned out, wasn't an alias for Lynne Addison, but a friend of Allie's from law school.

The second number was from a prepaid cell phone account. Since the phone, and the card to add minutes, had been purchased at a discount store, there was no way to trace it. The number had a Cincinnati area code—where Lynne and Jon were last spotted—but when Dean tried to call it, it was no longer in service.

In his pocket, his cell phone vibrated. He pulled it out and checked the number before flipping it open. "Hey there, darlin'," he said into the phone. "I was hoping you'd call."

"I have that information you asked for," Katherine said, as usual, getting right to the point. "Is this a bad time?"

"I need two minutes to get somewhere less crowded." He covered the mouthpiece as Allie set her tray of dirty glasses on the bar. "Mind if I take my break now?"

She shrugged, which he took as a yes. He rounded the bar and went outside, the cold hitting him like a right jab.

"Sorry 'bout that," he told Katherine as he hurried to his truck. "What did you find out?"

He climbed inside and started the ignition. He'd dug into Allie's past and kept her under surveillance the past three days, but hadn't discovered anything new except that she speed-walked four miles every morning—no matter how cold—and if her stopping by the local bakery afterward was any indication, had a serious sweet tooth. Neither of which led him to Lynne and Jon Addison.

"Allison Martin worked for the public defender's office a year before being offered a job at Hanley, Barcroft, Blaisdell and Littleton," Katherine said.

"I knew that. Guess the bigwigs there had been impressed with the number of cases she'd won." Dean sure had been.

Katherine grunted. "Every case she won was a check mark in the loss column for the good guys—you know that, right?"

The good guys in this case being the NYPD. "Now don't take it personally. Besides, you have to admit, she was an excellent attorney. She'd been on the fast track for a partnership even before she took on Miles Addison as her client."

"I don't have to admit any such thing," Katherine said. "And if you know so much, why'd you ask me to check her background?"

"Because that's all I could find out—*her* background—when what I need to know is about the Miles Addison case."

"Not much to find out. From what I can tell, Allison Martin may have been right to take his case."

"Wasn't he accused of molesting a young boy?"

"Yeah, but it was a tough one to prosecute. For one thing, Addison had public sentiment on his side. He's successful, wealthy, handsome and intelligent. He's also a well-known name in New York. He serves on the boards of numerous charitable organizations, donating millions of dollars to those in need each year."

"Sounds like a real prince. So his popularity kept him from going to prison? Or was he really innocent?"

"You think I have a crystal ball or something? All I know is that there was no physical evidence, just the kid's word against Addison's. Addison claimed the boy's mother had been blackmailing him for the past six months, that she'd threatened to bring him on up these charges if he didn't pay her."

"He go to the cops?"

Katherine snorted. "Nah. Turns out at the time all of this happened he was debating a run for public office. He figured if he didn't pay her, she'd force her son to lie and he didn't want anything to derail his ambitions. Phone records indicated the mother called Addison at his office twice a month for the preceding six months, which supported his claim. He also had bank slips showing large withdrawals on the same dates as the phone calls. He maintained that after she called, he'd get the money—in cash as per her orders—and meet her at a bar in Brooklyn. The defense team even got one of the bartenders who worked there to testify he saw Addison and the mother together at least twice."

"If he was paying her, how'd he end up in court?"

"I guess she asked for more than he was willing to give. When he balked, she threatened to tell not only his wife what he'd allegedly done but also the newspapers. He realized how much power he'd given her. He told her he wasn't giving her another cent and he just had to have faith that the truth would win out. The next day, the charges were filed."

"Sounds like Allie had more than enough evidence to prove there was reasonable doubt at the trial."

His comment was met with silence. "'Allie'?"

Katherine finally asked. "You're not getting too friendly with this girl, are you, Dean?"

He tugged on his left ear. "You know me. I'm playing my part."

"I hope so," she muttered. "But you're right about *Ms. Martin* proving reasonable doubt. After she cross-examined the mother on the stand, it looked as if the woman had set Addison up. If you ask me, the prosecution rushed the case to trial. They had no physical evidence so it came down to the kid's word against Addison's. It took them three hours of deliberation before acquitting him."

He drummed his fingers on the steering wheel. "Do you think Addison really *was* innocent?"

"Anything's possible," Katherine said. "And it's equally possible he was guilty."

That was why Dean had wanted more information about the case. He needed to know what Miles Addison was capable of. Robin had told Nolan her son-in-law was dangerous, and if that was true, Dean had to find out how many resources Addison had. How far he'd go to get his wife and son back.

He needed to keep Lynne and Jon safe once he found them.

He thanked Katherine for her help, promised he'd be careful, and then shut the ignition off and got out. So now he knew how the case against Addison had gone down. Too bad it didn't prove anything. He shoved his hands into his pockets and ducked his head against the wind. He still didn't know why Allie had defended the man—because she'd believed him innocent? Because she'd wanted a tough case to prove her worth? And it sure didn't give her motive for hiding Lynne and Jon.

Unless there was more to the story.

He pushed open the door to The Summit with enough force for it to bang against the inside wall. Several heads turned his way but he ignored the patrons.

Worse than being wrong or not solving the case was the idea of walking out on Allie. Leaving her alone with her denial about Richie and her savior tendencies left a bitter taste in his mouth.

He needed to remember the number one lesson of undercover work: don't get involved.

"IF YOU DON'T WANT TO believe what's happening under your nose," Dean told Allie over an hour later, "that's your business. But I think you should be careful."

"Are we still talking about Richie?" He nodded as she unloaded empty beer bottles and a dirty wineglass off her tray. "You're the second person to give me that excellent advice this week."

"What do you mean?"

She tucked her hair behind her ear. "Kelsey. She's… concerned about my hiring you."

He kept his expression carefully blank. "Her husband doesn't trust me—"

"That has nothing to do with it. Kelsey's not swayed by Jack. Or at least, not much. She's the most independent person I know. *She* doesn't trust you." Allie met his eyes. "And she doesn't think I should trust you, either."

Shit. "What about you? Do you trust me?"

"I'm not sure," she admitted. "I trust you to do

your job. So far you've been nothing but an asset to my business."

He almost smiled at her thinking of The Summit's bottom line. He put the empty beer bottles in the recycling bin. "I've only worked for you two days."

"Three if we include Saturday, which is already one day longer than either of the previous two bartenders I hired."

"I'm not going to leave you hanging," he said even though that's exactly what was going to happen. He already had a replacement bartender lined up for when the job was over.

Someone Allie really could count on.

She crumpled up a few paper napkins. "That's still to be decided, isn't it?"

Damn, why couldn't she accept him for who he said he was?

What the hell was he doing wrong?

At the end of the bar, the same gray-haired man who'd been sitting there last week when Dean first walked into The Summit, raised his empty glass. Dean pulled a beer and took it down to him as Allie threw away napkins behind the bar.

He needed to figure out how to play this. How to work this to his advantage.

"I thought we were friends," he said when he came back. "Wasn't that what you wanted? For us to be friends?"

She jerked one shoulder. "I was wrong."

"So you'll trust Richie, the drug addict—"

"Recovering drug addict."

"—but not me?"

It bugged him only because it compromised his cover.

She studied him. He waited for her to smile. To tell him of course she trusted him.

But she just picked up the tray and walked away.

Well, Allie didn't have to trust him, to like him, for him to get the information he needed.

But it would make his job a lot easier.

One of the braver college kids approached Allie as she cleaned off the table the couple had vacated. He said something to her and she laughed, tossing her hair over her shoulder. Dean's eyes narrowed.

The kid she'd turned on the charm for looked as hopeful as a tyke on Christmas Eve. Like if Allie stuck a bow on her head, his holiday would be complete.

Poor sap didn't have a clue. Dean would have to save him.

He tossed the rag down and strode over to them as the kid was saying "—done, we could maybe get together?"

"You're out of your league," Dean said before Allie could respond to the bumbling come-on. "Head on back to your friends before you humiliate yourself any further."

The kid swallowed, his Adam's apple bobbing. "I…I just thought—"

"No one blames you for dreaming big," Dean said as he put his arm around the youth's shoulders and steered him away from Allie. "How about a round on the house for you and your buddies, to take away the sting?"

He slapped the kid's shoulder hard enough to make him stumble forward. The student took the hint and kept walking back to his buddies at the pool table.

Allie stood, her mouth open, her eyes wide. What do

you know? Dean had managed to surprise her. Maybe he hadn't lost his touch completely.

He winked and went back to the bar.

ALLIE'S HAND SHOOK so hard the glasses on the tray she held clinked together. She set it down before she could give in to the urge to throw it at Dean's smug head.

She slowly approached the bar. "What in the hell do you think you're doing?"

He filled a pitcher with beer. "Getting a round for loverboy and his friends."

She held her hair back with both hands. "Do I look like someone who can't take care of herself?"

He appraised her. She let go of her hair and crossed her arms. "From what I've seen," he said, flipping the dispenser off, "you take care of yourself just fine."

Warmth suffused her, but she wasn't about to be swayed by what had sounded like a sincere compliment. "Exactly. So why would you take it upon yourself to scare the crap out of some poor guy just for talking to me?"

He held up the pitcher. A moment later, one of the college kids came over and took the beer without making eye contact with either one of them.

"Listen," Dean said, wiping up a few drops of beer, "it would've been cruel of me to stand back and let the kid get his hopes up."

She slapped her hands on the bar and leaned forward. "I have plenty of practice deflecting unwanted advances. I didn't need your help. And didn't you promise me not ten minutes ago that you were going to mind your own business?"

The door opened and six more college kids walked in. While she appreciated the business the spring breakers brought in, she wished the bar was empty tonight so she could close up and go home.

Instead of having to deal with Dean. Or the possibility that he might be right about Richie.

"I wasn't butting into your business and I didn't set out to help you," Dean said, nodding at the newcomers. "I was helping the kid."

She blinked. "What?"

"Someone had to get him out of there before he decided he had a chance with you. Although you lay it on thick, we both know the only way you'd give a kid like him the time of day is if he needed to be saved." Dean grinned. "Or maybe adopted."

She didn't return his smile. Couldn't. Not when anger made her see red.

"So, not only am I stupid for not seeing supposed drug use by one of my employees, but I'm also what? A tease? Oh, I know. Maybe I'm a man-eater. Well, thank God you stopped me before I got my claws into that unsuspecting boy."

His grin slid away and he reached out as if to touch her. "Hey, I didn't mean—"

"Never mind," she said, stepping back. "This isn't the time or place for this, anyway." Her movements were jerky as she gestured toward the two guys standing at the other end of the bar. "You have work to do and so do I."

She crossed the room for her abandoned tray and carried it into the kitchen. No sooner had the door swung shut behind her than she went to the table, set the tray down with a clang and sank into a chair.

"You okay?" Richie asked. He stood at the sink, finishing up the dishes from dinner.

She sighed. "I'm fine. Just tired." She even tossed in an insincere smile.

At least she should get points for effort.

But Richie didn't seem to notice anything was off with her. He nodded, his eyes…vacant.

She linked her hands together in her lap. Damn Dean for making her question Richie. When he'd returned from the grocery store Monday with no receipt and no change—even though she knew he couldn't have spent all the money—she'd told herself not to be paranoid. But now she wasn't so sure. And he kept sniffing and twitching. His hands trembled as he set a cast-iron pan aside.

If Richie had started using again, she needed to find out now. Before he got in too deep.

Before she couldn't help him.

She stood and cleared her throat. "I know it's late notice, but do you think you could stick around tonight and mix up meatballs for tomorrow's menu?"

"Sure." He glanced at her over his shoulder. "But this time we use my grandma's recipe."

"What's wrong with my recipe?"

"Nothing." He pulled the plug from the sink and dried his hands before folding the towel. "Except for that one batch when you tossed in too much sea salt."

"Now you can't hold that against me. It's not like I served them to paying customers."

"You're going to love Grandma's meatballs." He unfolded the towel, then folded it again. "Trust me."

Her breath hitched. She wanted to trust him. About way more than meatballs. "Sounds good. Let me check to make sure Dean has everything under control in the bar and we'll get started."

Since she needed her tray—and because she hadn't meant to bring it into the kitchen in the first place—she picked it up. Pushed through the door.

Was she crazy to think Richie would jeopardize the life he'd built for himself? After all, he was more than happy to work late, and his job meant so much that he became personally invested in meatballs, for God's sake. They'd even been discussing the possibility of him taking over the cooking twice a week to give Allie a break. And he'd told her that one day, when he'd saved up enough, he'd like to attend culinary school. Maybe open a restaurant.

Her fingers tightened on the tray. Richie wouldn't risk his future, everything he'd worked so hard to achieve these last few months of staying clean. She'd bet on it.

She went back into the kitchen to tell him to go home, that they'd make the meatballs tomorrow morning, but the room was empty. And his coat was gone.

She frowned. Maybe he'd gone outside for…for what? It was fifteen degrees out. And if he'd had to use the restroom, why take his coat?

Unless there was something in his coat he needed.

Her throat clogged. She was going to have to confront Richie whether she wanted to or not.

CHAPTER EIGHT

THOUGH SHE FELT DEAN'S intense gaze on her, Allie managed to ignore him for the rest of the night. Not an easy task, since Noreen only worked until they stopped serving food at ten on weeknights and Allie had the combined jobs of waitress and busboy, forcing her to work in the bar instead of hiding in the kitchen until closing time. Luckily, both she and Dean were kept busy when the crowd grew to a decent size.

Other than Dean trying to catch her eye, and her stomach twisting with nerves about talking to Richie later, the evening went smoothly. There were no fights, no one had to be cut off, and best of all, "Hotel California"—a song she'd heard way too many times since buying the bar—wasn't played even once on the jukebox.

After last call, the bar slowly emptied. Carla Owens, a pretty nurse who sometimes met a group of friends there after her shift at the hospital ended, was last to leave. Alone.

That was surprising because Carla had spent the past two hours flirting with Dean.

It hadn't seemed to bother the cowboy. Guess it only bugged him when Allie flirted.

He was such a hypocrite.

While Dean locked up after the last customer, Allie took off for the kitchen.

"You running away from me, Allie?" he asked, stopping her in her tracks. She shivered at the low timbre of his voice. But it was the amusement in it, the challenge, that made her turn.

"No. Richie's waiting for me."

"Really?" Dean walked toward her, his strides unhurried, his expression blank. "And why is that?"

She stepped to the side and set a chair on top of a table. Just to give her hands something to do. "I'm going to talk to him about what you…your concerns about him."

He took the next chair from her and set it on the table. "You believe me?"

She concentrated on brushing a piece of lint off her sleeve. "I want to ask him a few questions. To ease my own mind."

"And you were going to confront him alone?"

Her shoulders stiffened. Even though Dean sounded calm, she could tell he thought that was a stupid idea. Well, it was *his* idea, damn it, so he could can it.

"I'm not confronting him. I'm just going to talk to him."

"I'll go with you."

"That's not necessary. I can handle this on my own."

"See now, here's the thing. I know you can handle it. But if I'm right and Richie is using, you can't be sure how he'll react to you…easing your mind about him."

"Richie would never hurt me. He'd never hurt anyone."

Dean studied her as if wondering whether she really was as naive as she sounded.

But her naïveté was all in the past. And while she'd willingly give Richie the benefit of the doubt, she wasn't about to let him take advantage of her.

"I'm sure Richie's a regular old pussycat when he's sober," Dean said. "But if I'm right and he is high, I'd feel better knowing you weren't questioning him alone. Besides, you're confronting him because of what I told you. I have no problem standing up and letting him know I'm the one behind the accusation."

"Definitely not. I don't want him to feel accused, or worse, cornered."

Dean shifted and hooked his thumbs in his belt loops. "What if I apologized?"

"To Richie?"

"To you."

"For what, exactly?" Yeah, she was messing with him. But no more than he deserved. She thought he'd blow it off or say he was sorry for making her mad. Most men, in her experience, never knew what they were apologizing for half the time.

He bowed his head for a moment, but when he raised it again, didn't look angry. Just…sheepish. "For sticking my nose where it didn't belong. For acting as if you needed help with Richie and that college Romeo. And for making it seem as if you were some sort of cheap flirt."

"Well." She cleared her throat. Holy cow, he was good. When she met those intense green eyes of his, she wanted to believe he meant every word. "I guess I'd accept your apology. *If* you meant it."

"Fair enough." He rubbed his chin and then let his hand drop. "To be honest, I'm not sorry I told you my suspicions about Richie. But I am sorry you have to do what you're about to. I'm sorry you've been let down by someone you care for."

"And the thing about my flirting?"

A muscle jumped in his jaw. "Do you really want to know why I sent that drooling kid on his way?" he asked quietly. "How I felt to see you smiling at him? Or when he put his hand on you?"

Her throat went dry. The last thing she wanted was to admit the attraction between them was real. She needed to ignore it for as long as possible. Maybe even forever.

"Apology accepted," she said.

He seemed almost as relieved as she was.

"I'd like to sit in while you talk to Richie."

Although he'd made it a statement, she knew what it really was. A question. And she couldn't help but appreciate that he was asking.

"Fine. But let me do the talking."

"Sure thing, boss."

She inhaled and put her hand on the door, but couldn't push it open. What if she was wrong? What if there was some reasonable explanation for Richie's odd behavior?

She sighed. And what if she didn't confront him? What if she pretended not to see what was in front of her?

Like with the Addison case.

She couldn't let that happen. Not again. She'd already paid too high a price for believing in Miles Addison. She wouldn't make the same mistake twice.

Dean placed his hand on the small of her back, the

warmth of his fingers seeping into her skin. "It's okay," he said into her ear, his breath warm as it caressed her cheek. "I'm right behind you."

And why that meant as much to her as it did, she'd never know.

She pulled her shoulders back and entered the kitchen. Richie was taking a pan of meatballs from the oven.

"Richie, what—"

He spun around, losing his grip on the large pan in the process. It crashed to the floor. Grease splattered and meatballs rolled everywhere, some crushed under the heavy container.

"I'm sorry, Allie." Richie tossed the pot holders onto the counter and dropped to his knees in the midst of the mess. "I'll clean it," he said, sweeping meatballs into a pile with his forearm. "It'll only take a minute."

"Those are still hot," she said, avoiding as much of the grease as possible as she crossed to him. "Why don't we let them cool first, then I'll help you? After all, you wouldn't have dropped them if I hadn't startled you."

Richie blinked up at her. "Yeah, yeah. Good idea."

She helped him to his feet and tugged him away from the chaos. "I thought you were mixing the meatballs tonight. Not cooking them."

"I wanted you to taste one." His quick grin made him look five years younger. "So you'd know Grandma's were the best."

"I'm sure they're great," she said as he wiped his hands down the front of his jeans. Even though the kitchen was a comfortable temperature, sweat beaded his upper lip. "Richie, I was hoping I could talk to you before you head home."

"Sure, sure. No problem." His eyes widened and Allie turned to see what had spooked him.

She ground her back teeth together. Dean had so far kept his word by not speaking, but his body language said plenty. He stood by the door, his large arms crossed, his hat partially shading his hooded eyes.

"Dean, why don't you get yourself something to drink?" she asked, although from the way he raised his eyebrows, he understood it wasn't a suggestion. "And there are plenty of leftovers in the fridge if you want to heat up a late dinner for yourself."

Their eyes locked as they silently battled. She didn't so much as blink. After all, facing down hostile witnesses, egomaniac judges and jurors had all been a day's work for her not too long ago. No way was some smooth-talking, stubborn cowboy going to get her to back down.

He took his sweet time pushing away from the wall and moseying on over to the fridge. If she hadn't seen him punch Harry the other night, she would've sworn the man only had one speed: slow-enough-to-drive-a-person-insane.

"Is everything okay, Allie?" Richie asked. "Am I in trouble?"

"Everything's fine." She even added a smile, but figured it came across more like a grimace. Not that Richie seemed to notice. He was too busy sending nervous glances Dean's way.

She sat down. "Richie," she said, when he remained standing, staring as Dean straightened from the refrigerator, a can of soda in his hand. "Richie." This time louder. "Please sit down."

His body twitched as if someone had shot electricity through him, but he finally sat opposite her. "What's up?"

Her throat tightened. Dean had been right—Richie was using again. His pupils were dilated and he kept fidgeting. Picking at a small ding in the tabletop. Tossing his head to get the hair out of his eyes. And he'd hooked his foot around the leg of the chair next to him and kept pushing it away and pulling it back again.

She clasped her hands in her lap so she wouldn't reach over and shake the living hell out of him. How long had he been using? How could he do this to himself? What had happened to send him back to the drugs?

And the biggest, scariest question of all: Why hadn't she noticed before?

"I need to ask you something," she told him, trying to hold his gaze. "And all I want is for you to be honest. Whatever your answer, I hope it's the truth."

"Yeah, yeah. Okay." He scratched his arm, his eyes flicking to Dean, then to her again. "What is it?"

She linked her hands on top of the table. "Are you using again?"

He reared back. "No." But his voice shook. "I'm clean. You know that."

"You've been acting strange," she said with a calmness she didn't feel. "You've been late for work several times in the past few weeks—"

"I told you, I had a flat tire that one day." He ran a trembling hand over his face. "And that other time, my alarm didn't go off."

And she was such a fool, she'd believed him both times. "Plus," she continued, "you look terrible. You're pale and sweating and—"

"I've been sick," he cried, slamming his hands on the table. "You know I've been sick. But I'm feeling better. I'm sure tomorrow I'll be fine. And I won't be late again, I swear."

"I saw you using," Dean said. Though the words were spoken softly, they seemed to fill the room.

Richie jumped to his feet, knocking his chair backward. "You're a damn liar."

Dean set his soda can on the table. "Sit down."

"He's lying," Richie repeated, this time looking at Allie as if willing her to believe him. Begging her to. "I'm clean. I swear it." He looked ready to cry.

She could relate.

Allie stood, ignoring how unsteady her legs were. "Let me help you. Sit down so we can discuss—"

Richie kicked the chair. It skidded through the meatballs and banged into the counter. "You either believe him or me."

Her heart pounded heavily. She stepped toward Richie, stopping when Dean took hold of her arm. She tried to shake him off but he tightened his grip.

"We'll get you back in rehab," she told Richie. He looked at her with such anger and contempt, she shivered. "Your job is still secure. And once you come back, you—"

"Forget it," he snarled. He crossed the room and snatched his coat off the hook on the wall. "I'm not going to rehab and I don't need your help." He opened the door. "I thought you were different," he whispered roughly. "I thought I could trust you."

And then he walked out and slammed the door.

She jerked out of Dean's hold and, willing her tears away, walked to the closet for the broom and dustpan. Feeling Dean's gaze on her, she leaned the broom against the counter, picked up the baking dish and set it on the counter before sweeping meatballs into the dustpan.

She emptied them into the trash, biting her trembling lower lip when Dean touched her shoulder. "Hey, you—"

"Don't," she muttered, shrugging his hand off. She bowed her head and struggled to swallow past the lump in her throat. "Don't…please…don't ask me if I'm okay. Or tell me I did the right thing."

"All right," he said. Then he took the broom and walked over to the mess.

She frowned. "What are you doing?"

He swept some of the meatballs into a pile. "You spend a lot of time cleaning up other people's messes. Tonight, you don't have to do it alone."

THE NEXT MORNING, Dean spent close to five minutes staring at the pink, heart-shaped wreath on Allie's door while he waited for her to let him in. He'd rung the bell for the seventh time when the door opened.

He'd obviously woken her. She wore a pair of baggy gray sweatpants, a faded Columbia University sweatshirt and a pair of fuzzy red socks. Her hair was a mess.

And she was still the most beautiful thing he'd ever seen.

His fingers tightened on the two plastic grocery bags he held. "Morning," he said, working to keep his voice even. Not an easy task when she looked all warm and sleepy, as if the only thing she wanted was to crawl back into bed.

Which, when he thought about it, didn't sound like a bad idea.

She yawned. "Hi. Everything okay?"

"Fine. A bit cold…" Yeah, just a bit. He'd lost feeling in his fingers three minutes ago.

She blinked slowly. "Sorry. Come on in."

He took his hat off as he stepped inside, careful not to brush against her. She closed the door and then leaned against it. A black, long-haired cat meowed and wound around his legs.

Dean set his bags down and scratched behind the cat's ears. She purred, lifting her head and closing her eyes. "What's her name?" he asked.

"Hmm?"

He bit back a grin. He'd come here hoping to get more information about Allie, and he'd already learned something new. She was not a morning person.

Not that he thought that insight would help him finish his job, but it didn't hurt to know she wasn't always at the top of her game. And part of the reason he was there was to try and catch her off guard, find out who the number from her cell phone he and Nolan hadn't been able to trace belonged to. A friend? An ex-lover?

Or Lynne Addison?

"Your cat's name," he said. "I'm assuming she has one."

"Of course. It's Persephone." Allie yawned again. "I don't mean to be rude, but what are you doing here?"

He picked up the bags and straightened. Held them up as Persephone meowed again and nudged his leg with her head. "I'm making you breakfast."

"What? Why?"

"You've fed me for almost a week. I thought I should return the favor."

She frowned, looking adorably confused. "But… that's a perk of your job."

"Dinner Sunday night wasn't."

"Still, you don't need—"

"I want to." He stepped forward so that only a foot separated them. Wariness entered her expression. "Besides, I thought maybe you could…use a friend. After what happened last night."

Her mouth popped open and she acted as if he'd thrust the bags at her and demanded she make *him* breakfast.

"I really need coffee," she muttered.

She shuffled away and around a corner, Persephone giving chase. Still holding his hat, Dean rubbed his chin with the back of his hand, noticing a wooden bench, like an old church pew, against the wall behind him. He tossed his hat on the glossy, dark wood, then sat. After taking off his boots and setting them on a heavy mat under the bench, he stood and laid his coat down. With the bags in hand, he went in search of his unwilling host.

And if he felt like the biggest jerk for using her innate goodness and her worry about Richie to worm his way not only inside her home, but inside her head as well, he'd get over it.

The end always justified the means.

When he found her in the small kitchen, he pursed his lips. Bent at the waist, her ass in the air, her head resting in her folded arms on the counter, she was muttering at the coffeepot to hurry up. Beside her were two mugs and a container of some sort of flavored creamer. Persephone, sitting at Allie's feet, purred loudly.

He cleared his throat. "Does talking to the pot like that make it work faster?"

"I hope so."

He set his bags on the table and started unloading them. "I hope you like pancakes. I make my mother's secret recipe."

She grunted. Allison Martin—classy, stylish, always put together, always one step ahead of everyone—just grunted at him.

Was it any wonder he got such a big kick out of her?

"Hallelujah," she breathed at last. She poured coffee into one of the mugs, then added at least as much creamer. He grimaced. Why ruin a perfectly good cup of coffee by making it taste like sugar cookies or some other crap?

She wrapped both hands around her mug, lifted it to her face and inhaled.

"Are you sniffing your coffee?" he asked.

"Please. I'm having a moment here." She sipped, her eyelids drifting shut in apparent ecstasy.

And damn if he didn't want to see if *he* could put that look on her face. Even if he couldn't, he bet they'd have a lot of fun trying.

After a few more sips, she poured him a cup. "Do you want anything in yours?"

"Black's fine." When she handed it to him, he purposely allowed his fingers to linger over hers. As a test. For both of them. "Thanks," he said.

She swallowed and he noticed she curled her fingers into her palm. She nodded at the groceries on the table. "I'm fine, you know. You don't have to do this."

"I want to."

Last night she'd been so upset, she hadn't said a word after Dean told her he'd stick around and help her clean up. But it wasn't her silence that had bothered him. That had him wanting to take her in his arms and tell her that no matter what happened, everything would work out. That made him want to protect her.

It was because she'd seemed so vulnerable. So crushed.

She opened a can of cat food and dumped it into Persephone's dish, then filled the other dish with fresh water and washed her hands. "Well, since you're sort of insisting and all," she said, drying them on a tea towel, "what can I do to help?"

"I need half of these chopped." He tossed her a small bag of pecans, impressed by her one-handed catch. "Where are your mixing bowls?"

She picked up a cutting board and knife and gestured to her left. "Bottom cupboard."

By the time he found the bowls, she'd set out measuring cups and spoons.

"How are you holding up?" he asked.

She poured the pecans into a large glass measuring cup before scooping out exactly half onto the cutting board. "I'm fine."

He crumpled the plastic bags and set them on a chair. "You seemed pretty upset last night."

"I just…I don't want to talk about it."

"No talking." He saluted her with a banana. "No problem."

She set to work chopping pecans, one nut at a time, into tiny, even pieces.

"They don't have to be quite that…perfect," he said.

"Is it hurting anything if I do it this way?" Her chilly tone told him that was a trick question that had no right answer.

"No?"

"Then I guess I'll keep doing it the way I want."

And if he'd said yes, she would've challenged him on why the pecans had to be chopped a certain way. See? No right answer.

He poured buttermilk into the large bowl and added three eggs and some vanilla before whisking them together with a fork. Patience was all a part of the game, of his job.

Not that he'd have to wait long. He'd been around Allie enough to know that she didn't stay quiet for long. At least not once she had her morning coffee. She always seemed to be engaged in conversation, be it with a customer, an employee or the guy who delivered the beer. She also had a bad habit of saying whatever was on her mind.

It was only a matter of time before she cracked. After all, he hadn't come here just to make pancakes.

He stirred the dry ingredients together in the small bowl. Dumped the rest of the pecans back into the bag so he could melt butter in the glass measuring cup in the microwave.

"I feel so stupid," Allie blurted.

Damn, he loved being right.

He took the butter from the microwave and set it on the table before adding the dry ingredients to the larger bowl. "One thing you're not is stupid."

Finished with the pecans, she brushed her hands together. "I didn't know Richie had started using again."

Dean mixed the ingredients together and added the butter and chopped pecans. "It's hard to see things we don't want to see."

That he knew from firsthand experience.

"You saw it," Allie groused, making it sound like an accusation.

"I'm not emotionally invested in what happens to Richie. Sometimes you have to step away from a situation to be able to see it clearly." He handed her three bananas. "Want to slice these for me?"

"Bananas in pancakes?"

"You'll love them. Trust me."

While she worked on the bananas, he found a large skillet and set it on the stove, turned the flame on underneath it.

"So, your theory on stepping back...is that your educated opinion? Or are you speaking from experience?"

He added butter to the pan, listening to it sizzle as it melted. "Experience. Definitely experience."

"I WAS MARRIED," Dean said, his back still to her.

"I know," Allie replied. He glanced at her over his shoulder. "Remember? Sunday when Jack was interrogating you, you told him you were divorced."

Dean nodded and turned back to the stove. She sipped her coffee. It was lukewarm, so she got up and refilled both their cups. The scent of melted butter filled her kitchen. Dean poured batter into the hot pan and then picked up the cutting board with the sliced bananas.

This entire…thing…was too weird. And growing weirder by the moment. The last person she'd ever expected to see on her doorstep was Dean Garret. And yet there he stood, in her kitchen, big as life. It was surreal. To be honest, she should be freaked out. She hadn't brushed her hair or her teeth yet, for God's sake.

But she couldn't muster the energy to care.

She took down two plates and set them by the stove, then added cream to her coffee. "Divorce is never easy," she said, a not-so-subtle nudge to get him talking again.

He pressed some banana slices into the pancakes. "You divorced?"

"Well, no—"

"And your parents have been together how long?"

"Thirty-five years," she admitted, leaning back against the counter, her feet crossed. Persephone curled up next to her. "But half of all marriages end in divorce, and I have friends who've been through it."

He smirked. "Darlin', having friends who get divorced isn't quite the same as going through it…or your parents splitting up." He expertly flipped the pancakes.

She kept her hands wrapped around her mug. She knew if she touched him like she wanted to, he'd shrug her off. "That must've been rough."

He slid the cooked pancakes onto a plate before adding

more batter to the pan. "My mom made these pancakes on special occasions, like our birthdays or Christmas. And the last day of school. She always said the last day was more cause to celebrate than the first day."

"Smart mom."

"She is at that." He added the bananas and then went to the table and poured maple syrup into the measuring cup, placing it in the microwave to warm. "The only other time she made them was the morning she told us Dad had moved out. There was no warning, just…Dad's gone and he won't be coming back."

"You had no idea they were having problems?"

"If they were—and the fact they started divorce proceedings the next day tells me they were—we didn't know it."

"How old were you?"

"Eleven." He finished the pancakes. Handed her both plates to carry to the table while he grabbed the syrup. "Ryan was nine and Sammy was six."

She set the plates down, wondering what he'd been like at that age. Had he ever really been young and carefree? Or was he always serious and contained? Did his parents' divorce force him to take on that protective outer shell? And if so, what did he think he needed protection from now?

"How did you deal with it?" she asked, placing glasses, forks and napkins on the table before getting a carton of orange juice out of the fridge.

He snorted. "We had no clue what she was telling us. What she meant by they weren't in love anymore. That Dad had decided to take a job in Austin, but we could still visit him. Maybe stay at his new house for a week or two during the summer." He added whole pecans to the syrup and pulled her chair out for her, waiting for her to sit before he did the same. "It wasn't until about a year later that I realized all the signs were there." He tapped his fist against the table. "I'd just been blind to them."

His voice was flat, his face expressionless. She knew discussing this was hard on him. And even though he probably didn't want her sympathy, she couldn't help but offer it in some small way.

She covered his clenched hand with her own. "Give yourself a break. You were just a kid."

He slid his hand out from under hers and poured syrup over his stack of pancakes before passing it to Allie. "It happened again when I was older. In my own marriage."

"I don't understand. What happened again?"

He picked up his fork and cut into his pancakes, but didn't eat. "My not noticing what was right in front of my face. Not wanting to see how unhappy my wife was, so I could pretend that everything was all right."

After a long silence, Allie turned to her plate of pancakes and began to eat for lack of anything helpful to say. They were light and fluffy, and the bananas added a touch of sweetness while the pecans added crunch. She hesitated and then finally said, "I hope you don't mind me saying this, but I can't believe your ex-wife wouldn't stay married to you just for these pancakes."

One side of his mouth quirked in that half grin she found so appealing. Some of the knots in her stomach loosened. She didn't want to see him morose. She had that emotion covered, thank you very much.

"Actually, I don't think I ever cooked for her. Something else I screwed up."

Allie took a sip of juice. "Wow. I'm impressed."

"Don't try and sweet-talk me. My mother would skin me if I gave out her secret recipe."

"Not with the pancakes." Although she did wish she'd been awake enough to pay attention while he'd mixed up the batter, so she could make them herself. "With the amazing breadth of your shoulders. How do you manage to stay upright carrying around all that guilt and responsibility?"

He narrowed his eyes. "Guilt has nothing to do with it. I take accountability for my actions. That's all."

"Doesn't your ex-wife get to be accountable? After all, you didn't marry yourself."

"Marrying her wasn't my first mistake. Getting her pregnant was."

CHAPTER NINE

ALLIE CHOKED ON HER COFFEE. "You have a child?" she sputtered.

Pain he thought he'd blocked years ago resurfaced, threatening to bring him to his knees. "No. He was stillborn."

"He?"

His mouth tightened. "Robert James. He would've turned nine this past summer."

"Dean," she said, laying her hand on his again, "I'm so sorry."

He pulled back and picked up his fork. Ate a bite of pancake even though it now tasted like sawdust. "My marriage never should've happened. Jolene and I dated casually for a few months. I wasn't looking for anything serious and, at the time, didn't think she was, either." He stared at the kitchen wall above Allie's head. "Two months after we stopped seeing each other, I enlisted. When she told me she was pregnant, I was so shocked, all I could think about was myself."

"That seems pretty normal for a young man."

He forced himself to finish his breakfast and drink

his juice. Anything to keep from looking at Allie as he admitted his greatest failure.

"Even through the shock, I knew what the right thing to do was." He stood and carried his dishes to the sink. "I'd never met Jo's parents, didn't know when her birthday was or her favorite ice cream. And I didn't love her. But none of that mattered. So I said, 'Well, I guess we'd better get married.'" He'd been such an idiot. "At the time, I thought she was disappointed because I didn't have a ring for her. I recently figured out it was my piss-poor proposal that did it."

"There's no right or way wrong to act when something like that is dropped in your lap."

Allie's kind words set his teeth on edge. The last thing he wanted was her sympathy. Or her understanding. Not when he didn't deserve either.

Not when he was opening up to her in an attempt to get her to do the same.

"Maybe not," he agreed. "But even though I was young, I could've handled it better. I *should've* handled it better." He tapped his fist against his thigh. "We got married and she came with me to San Diego for boot camp two weeks later. We were there three months, and when I got my orders to go to Afghanistan, I started thinking we'd be okay."

He'd been desperate to make his marriage work. Because somehow he'd come to love his unborn child more than anything.

"The shock had worn off by then," he continued, "and I was excited to prove I could do a better job of parenting than my old man. I swore I wasn't going to shuffle my kid from house to house. Or worse, forget I had a child if the marriage failed—like my dad. Once he remarried and became a stepfather to his new wife's kids, his own three sons no longer existed." Dean shrugged. "Jolene and I had decided she should move back in with her parents while I was overseas. I was on a recon mission when she went to the hospital. She hadn't felt the baby move all day." He exhaled heavily. "They induced labor. Jolene had to go through childbirth knowing our son was already dead. And I wasn't with her."

She covered his hand with hers. "Even if you'd been there," Allie said gently, "there wasn't anything you could have done."

He sat back, pulling away from her touch. "I could've seen my son. Held him at least once. Jo was so crushed, she had the funeral two days later. I didn't get home until that night."

And that was a betrayal he'd never be able to forgive.

"I'm so sorry, Dean," Allie whispered.

"The baby was the only thing that held us together. But for some reason—stubbornness or pride—we stuck it out for five years." He rotated his coffee cup and sighed. "Jolene wanted another baby but I…I couldn't do that. When she asked for a divorce, I was relieved. I told myself she was too needy. But all she wanted was a real marriage and a family. Neither of which I was willing to give her."

"Maybe…" Allie stared at the remains of her breakfast, a frown on her face as if she was searching for the right words. "Maybe you weren't *able* to give her either of those." She raised her head. "You made a mistake, but you can't keep punishing yourself for it."

He forced a smile. "It all worked out for the best. Jolene remarried. She even has a one-year-old daughter."

"So you and Jolene still keep in touch?"

He shoved his cup away. "Not really."

"Then how did you know…"

"The man she married, the father of her child, is my brother."

SHOCKED, ALLIE SAT BACK. "I'm not sure what to say…. Those first few family get-togethers must've been weird."

"I wouldn't know," Dean said, picking up an empty grocery bag and shaking it in front of Persephone. The cat leaped back, then crouched, ready to make her move when he shook it again. "The last time I saw my family was two Christmases ago."

"What does that mean? You all haven't been together since then?"

Persephone pounced on the bag and Dean swept it— and the cat—from side to side. "I'm sure they've gotten together. They just haven't invited me."

Uh-oh. "What did you do?"

"What makes you think I did something?"

"Because you were upset. And often times when people are hurt, they lash out."

He straightened and laid his hands flat on the table, his expression etched with anger and regret. "How the hell did they think I was going to react? I'd just been discharged from the marines and was looking forward to spending Christmas with my family for the first time in five years. Except, when I get to my mother's house, I find out my brother's not only been seeing my ex-wife for the past seven months, but my entire family knew and no one bothered to tell me."

Oh, poor Dean. First he lost his son and then his family kept something like that from him? No wonder he had trust issues and moved from town to town. He couldn't go home. "Why the secrecy?"

"Guess they were worried about my reaction." He leaned back and crossed his arms. "So instead, they thought it'd be safer to spring it on me as I walked through the door. And then Ryan tells us all that Jolene's pregnant."

Allie winced. "They just dropped one bomb after another on you, didn't they?"

Dean laughed but the sound was hollow. "You could say that. I was furious. I said some things I shouldn't have said, which set Ryan off, and the next thing I knew, I broke his nose and he split my lip." He opened and clenched his fist as if he'd punched his brother minutes ago instead of years. "We haven't spoken since."

She rested her elbows on the table. "Because you don't want to? Or because neither one of you knows how to make the first move?"

He shrugged. "At first I was too angry, but as time went by it became…easier…to avoid my family. Especially after Jolene had the baby."

"You've never even seen your niece?" Allie asked. The idea of not being with her own family for that long made her heartsick.

He gave his head a quick, jerky shake. "Sam e-mailed me a picture but I…I couldn't make myself open it."

Yes, he'd acted like an idiot with his brother and family, but she understood why. And it wasn't because his brother had fallen in love with Dean's ex-wife.

It was because Ryan and Jolene had what Dean and Jolene lost.

A child.

"It sounds to me as if you're punishing yourself," she said, ignoring the look he shot her. "By keeping away from your family, you're not just hurting them, you're hurting yourself."

"I'm not trying to hurt anyone."

"But…don't you miss them? Don't you want to meet your niece?"

She didn't think he was going to answer, but then he said, "I used to wonder if things might've worked out differently if I hadn't joined up. If I'd been with Jolene at the time…"

"What could you have done? It was out of your hands." Allie softened her tone as she added, "Do you honestly think if you'd still been in Texas your baby would've lived?"

He stabbed a hand through his hair. "No," he admitted helplessly, "but I can't help feeling responsible for the failure of my marriage. For not being able to give Jolene what she wanted most." He straightened his legs. "You and I are a pair, huh? Both trying to fix things that are out of our control."

She raised her eyebrows. "I'm out of the fixing-people game. I tried that once and it didn't work out so well for me."

"Really? Then why were you so upset about Richie?"

"I just…wish I'd recognized earlier that he needed help."

"So you're not trying to save him?"

"Absolutely not." Even if the little voice inside her head called her a liar.

"Good. You should be focusing on yourself, on your own life. You should be going after what you want, not worrying about everyone else."

"The last time I went after what I wanted I—" She clamped her lips together and pushed her plate away, her throat burning with unshed tears. "Never mind."

"No." He caught her by the wrist as she shoved her chair back. "Don't run. What happened? Why can't you put yourself first?"

She tried to pull away from him, but he wouldn't let go. "Because the last time I did," she said hoarsely, "I helped a pedophile go free."

HE WASN'T GOING TO FEEL bad about doing his job. About digging to find out what Allie was hiding. Not after he'd laid himself bare to her.

"I don't understand," Dean said. "What do you mean, you helped a pedophile?"

She tugged on her arm and he released her. She took her empty dishes to the sink. Kept her back to him. "Do you know why I chose to become a defense attorney?"

He stood and put the juice and butter in the fridge. "Too many episodes of *Matlock?*"

"No." She turned around, but her smile was sad. "Although I did admire how he went all out for his clients." She turned on the water and rinsed plates before putting them in the dishwasher. "It was because of my dad."

"Wait, didn't I hear your dad was the ex-police chief?" She nodded. "I would've thought he'd sway you to become a district attorney or something."

"He's pretty liberal minded, for a cop. He told me that while our legal system is one of the best out there, it's still far from perfect. But it couldn't work at all if both sides weren't represented." She closed the dishwasher and began filling the sink with water, adding a squirt of soap. "He says the concept of innocent until proven guilty couldn't be possible without lawyers—defense attorneys in particular. That lawyers are advocates, while justice is the responsibility of the judge and jury."

"And you believed defending the accused was the most important part of the system."

"I thought I could help more people as a defense attorney." She scrubbed the skillet, her mouth a thin line. "I started off so idealistic. And naive. As cliché as it sounds, I thought I could change the world."

He dried the skillet and set it on the counter. "That's a big order for one person, no matter how good the intent."

She drained the water and wrung out the dishcloth. "No kidding."

He poured the rest of the coffee into their mugs, adding cream to hers and handing it to her. "What happened?"

She tossed the dishrag into the sink, took the coffee in one hand and scooped up Persephone with the other. Allie sank into her seat, sitting sideways, her gaze on the floor as the cat curled up in her lap. "Winning became very important to me. Too important."

"There's nothing wrong with wanting to do your best."

She looked up, her expression bleak. "There is if winning cases becomes more important than helping your clients."

He pulled out the chair next to her and moved it so he sat with his knees touching hers. "I can't see you ever allowing that to happen."

"I couldn't, either." She set her cup down and stroked Persephone. He had no doubt it helped soothe Allie, too. "At first, I talked myself into believing working for the big firm would be the same as what I'd been doing. Except the pay was three times what I was making at the public defender's office."

"Sounds like a win-win situation."

"I thought so. And I was willing to do whatever it took to prove their faith in me wasn't wasted. After two years I was moved from associate to lead attorney. My goal was to make junior partner before I was thirty-five." She sat back, her expression one of self-disgust. "I started out wanting to work for the greater good, and ended up throwing it all away because of my ambition for a corner office."

"But you gave it up," he pointed out. "You realized you were no longer happy."

"I realized I was a fraud."

He didn't want to spook her by seeming too eager to hear what she had to say. And…well…he hoped she'd *want* to tell him.

"I won the biggest case of my career," she admitted.

He raised his eyebrows. "And that's a bad thing?"

"I didn't think so at first, even though I was representing a man accused of sexually abusing a child. I was…" She closed her eyes and swallowed. "God, I was excited by the challenge of it. He was a pillar of the community, a happily married man. And I believed he was innocent."

"You couldn't be a defense attorney—at least, not a successful one—if you only represented people you felt were innocent."

She nodded. "You're right. But I was morally opposed to representing people accused of sex crimes." She set the cat on the floor and got up to pace the short length of the room. "Until this case." The remorse in her voice made his chest hurt.

"But my client was guilty," she exclaimed, "and thanks to me, to my expert defense, he was allowed to go free. Dean," she said raggedly, "he hurt a little boy and I helped him get away with it."

"Hey, now…" Dean crossed to her, wrapped his arms around her because there was no way he could keep from touching her, comforting her. "You're not to blame for his crimes. You were doing your job—"

"That's just it. All I cared about was doing my job." She clutched him, her arms around his waist, her head on his chest. "I didn't care about finding out the truth, didn't even consider the possibility he could've been guilty."

Dean held her away from him. He hated that she was upset. Hated even more that he'd manipulated her into sharing what was obviously a source of great guilt and pain.

"Stop it," he said quietly. "You weren't the only one to believe him. He had everyone fooled, even his wife."

Allie pushed him back a step. "How do you know his wife was fooled?"

CHAPTER TEN

DEAN'S EYEBROWS DREW together as if he was trying to figure out what she was talking about. "You mentioned he was married. I just assumed his wife stood by him during the trial."

Her shoulders slumped. "You're right. She did."

He rubbed his hands up and down her arms. "You had evidence the guy was innocent, and a jury agreed. What makes you so sure he really was guilty?"

"The day after the trial ended," she said slowly, "the boy ended up in the hospital. He...he tried to kill himself."

Sympathy softened Dean's features. "That's not your fault," he said, cupping her face in his large hand. "You couldn't have known."

She pulled away from his touch. "That doesn't make it easier. That kid had no one to protect him. He's the one who needed help, not Miles. But it was my job to see only what I needed to see." She hugged her arms around herself. "And I was very good at my job."

"That boy could've had a number of reasons to hurt himself," Dean pointed out. "You can't be sure it's because your client abused him."

She began pacing again. She couldn't stand to be so

close to Dean, not when she felt so weak. Not when all she wanted was to wrap herself around him and never let go.

"You're right, but it was enough to make me wonder if Miles *had* been abusing him. To start to question my part in what happened." She put her chair back, straightened his and pushed it in as well. "A few days later, Miles hosted a party at his home. At the end of the night, as I was leaving, Lynne—Miles's wife—stopped me. She'd had too much to drink, so when she started babbling about how I was to blame, I figured she was drunk."

Allie shivered, remembering Lynne's despondence, hearing the anger and desperation in her voice. "But then she…she broke down. Started crying. She told me she'd never be able to get her son away from him now. That Jon would never be safe."

"You didn't mention this guy had a kid."

She crossed to the refrigerator and traced the heart in a drawing Emma had given her. "Jon was six."

Dean straightened, his expression hard. "You think his wife was trying to tell you he was abusing his own son?"

Tears formed in her eyes but she refused to let them fall. "I don't know. I was too shocked to even move. When Miles joined us, he joked about his wife not being able to hold her alcohol. I was ready to shrug the whole thing off—I wanted to shrug it off," she said shakily, remembering the moment. "But when I got home, I couldn't stop thinking about what Lynne had said." Allie walked to the sink, stared at the softly falling snow out the window. "And since I couldn't let my doubts go, I asked a friend of mine, a detective, to do a bit of digging."

Dean watched her steadily. Patiently. Warmth suffused her, settled in her stomach. Her response to him was so elemental, and undeniable. But was that enough to warrant her desire to open up to him? To trust him when she hadn't been able to trust her family?

She cleared her throat. "He discovered some things...things that made me realize how wrong I'd been—"

"How wrong *you'd* been? Jeez, Allie, give yourself a break."

"How can I?" she cried. "All I could think about was that boy Miles had molested, and if his own son was suffering the same abuse. I had to make things right."

Dean frowned, his gaze intense. "Make things right? How?"

She stared down into the sink. "Worrying about making another mistake wouldn't help me or my clients, so I quit my job. The rest you know."

"What happened to them?"

"Who?"

"The wife and kid?"

The nape of her neck prickled. His question seemed innocent, so why did she feel as if he was digging for something? Didn't he realize she'd already told him all her secrets?

Or at least the ones that were hers to share.

"I have no idea. I never saw Lynne Addison again."

SHE WAS LYING TO HIM.

During his years as a PI, plenty of people had lied

to him. So why did it make him so mad that she was doing it?

Dean fisted his hand. He wanted her to tell him the truth. He wanted to forget the job and stop all the games between them.

He wanted her to trust him.

He couldn't ask her about the phone call Lynne had made to her office the day she and Jon disappeared. He had to tread carefully. He'd almost slipped up once by mentioning how Addison's wife had stood by him, and Dean couldn't blow it now. Not when he was finally getting somewhere.

He'd gotten the confirmation he needed to prove he'd been right all along. Allie did know what happened to Lynne and Jon. He'd bet his reputation on it.

She may have given up on saving the world, but something told him she hadn't given up on saving the Addisons.

In his front pocket, his cell phone vibrated, but he ignored it. "You're not to blame," he told her as he walked over and stood next to her. He gently gripped her chin and lifted her face, forcing her to meet his eyes. "You're not to blame," he repeated, because she was too stubborn to see it herself. "Not for what he did to that boy and not for any abuse his kid might have suffered."

"It's just that…all I've ever wanted to do was help. But like with Richie, wanting to help wasn't enough." She rolled her eyes. "God, I hate whiners."

Dean dropped his hand. "You sound like someone who wants to make a difference. There's nothing wrong with that."

"It's hard to make a difference when you don't trust

yourself to make the right decisions." She glanced at him. "When you've lost your ability to trust in others."

Before he could analyze the movement, he swept her hair back. Once his fingers were intertwined with the silky strands, once he was close enough to feel the brush of her thighs against his, feel warmth, he couldn't back away. He curled his fingers in the hair at her neck.

"I don't think you've lost that ability," he said softly. "You trusted me."

When he would have removed his hand, she tilted her head so that he cupped her cheek. "I guess I'll have to wait to see if that was a smart move."

"Not trusting yourself because of an error in judgment isn't so smart. Seems to me you gave up a lot more than just your job because of that guy. You said I was punishing myself by staying away from my family, but what about you? When are you going to stop letting your mistake rule your actions?"

She reached up and squeezed his hand. "That cowboy insight of yours is right on target."

"I'm not sure about that." He linked his fingers with hers. "But a person's character shows up best when tested. And yours showed up big time."

She laughed softly, her warm breath caressing his cheek. His body tensed. In her eyes he saw the same desire he felt coursing through his veins.

He traced her jaw with the tip of his finger. Then he raked his fingers through her hair, combing the length of it before massaging her scalp. She made a mewling sound and her eyes drifted shut.

Every day for the past week he'd fought his attraction to her. But now, standing in her tiny kitchen—with her wearing ugly, shapeless sweats and no makeup—he wanted her more than ever.

Damn it all to hell.

She wrapped her free hand around his forearm, her other hand still gripping his. Sexy. And beautiful. She looked unsure and at the same time so hopeful. He'd be a first-class idiot if he walked away.

And a first-class asshole if he didn't.

Slowly—so slowly he had plenty of time to evade her—she closed the distance between them. Her breasts pressed against his chest and he flinched, unsure how long he'd be able to maintain control.

Unsure if he even wanted to control himself any longer. Not when giving in meant he might get the chance to kiss her again. To keep touching her.

"Remember when you said I need to start putting myself first?" She slid her hand up his arm, under the sleeve of his T-shirt, to wrap around his biceps. "Is that what you really think?"

"Yeah," he croaked. He shut his eyes and cleared his throat. She turned him inside out. "Yeah. I do."

She glanced up at him from under her lashes. "So, that means if I…want something…I should go after it?"

No. No, no, no. no. Hell no. "You should. Definitely."

"Good." She lowered their linked hands and, watching his face, pressed his open palm to her breast. "Because what I want," she whispered, "is for you to touch me."

He glanced at his hand on her. Jerked his gaze up so that he was looking over her head.

"Dean," she asked uncertainly, "do you want me?"

He pressed his free hand to the small of her back and rocked his hips against hers. Her eyes darkened at the unmistakable feel of his arousal.

How could he not want her? But he'd promised himself he wouldn't touch her. Wouldn't cross that line, not when so many lies were between them.

She slid her hands into his hair and totally blew what little control he had out of the water. "I want you, too."

ALLIE KISSED DEAN BEFORE she could change her mind.

His body stiffened and his mouth was unyielding under hers. The only way it could've been worse was if he'd turned his head at the last minute so she'd ended up kissing his cheek.

A tactic she'd used many times herself.

She fell back to her heels, her face on fire. She wished something would happen to distract him from this moment. A meteor shower right about now should do the trick.

She smiled ruefully. "Well, that was humiliating."

And the way he stared at her, his fierce expression, was unnerving. She dropped her hands to his shoulders and started to step back, but he tightened his hold. She frowned. "Wha—"

"I'm sorry."

She winced. She'd been wrong. Him apologizing for not wanting to kiss her was even worse than an evasive do-not-kiss-me maneuver.

Still, she did her best to salvage some pride. "You don't have anything to apologize for."

"Not yet," he said, cupping her breast through her

sweatshirt. His thumb brushed against her nipple and she caught her breath. "But I'm about to."

His mouth crushed hers, his tongue sweeping into her mouth. She moaned and wrapped her arms around his neck, pressing against him. He gently kneaded her breast. Her nipples tightened, rubbed against the material of her sweatshirt.

He kissed along her neck, and she dropped her head back to grant him better access. Her mind whirled when he scraped his teeth across the sensitive skin below her ear.

He kissed his way back up to her mouth, shoved his fingers into her hair and held her head still. She smoothed her own hands over his broad shoulders, down his arms and back up again. Frantic to touch him, to feel his skin, she tugged the hem of his shirt up and caressed his lower back.

He twitched and jumped, so that her fingers brushed his sides. She took the opportunity to skim her hands over his rib cage, trailing her nails down the flat panes of his stomach. He growled and yanked her to him, trapping her hands between them as he spun them so that he leaned against the counter.

She stood between his legs, his hands gripping her butt. He rolled her hips forward and she arched against him.

He spun them again. With Dean's mouth on hers, his body pressed against hers, she didn't care that the hard edge of the counter dug into her spine or that she was pawing at him as if she'd go insane.

All she cared about was him. She wanted more.

She brushed her palm down the length of him. He

swore gutturally, gripping her upper arms as if to hold her still.

That was such a crazy thought, she couldn't help but smile. "It's okay," she told him, "I won't hurt you."

But he didn't return her smile. If anything, his expression darkened. "I don't want to hurt you, either."

She wasn't sure if she'd heard him right, but then he kissed her again, and in one smooth move, he'd stripped her sweatshirt over her head and tossed it aside. The cool air in the kitchen washed over her heated skin.

She raised her arms to cover herself but he just looked at her. Her heart hammering, she slowly lowered her arms.

Dean's breathing was uneven as he skimmed the tip of one finger down her left breast. She shivered.

"You are the most beautiful woman I've ever seen." He cupped her breasts in his hands, rubbed the rough pads of his thumbs over her skin. "And that's the honest truth."

He bent his head, took one nipple in his mouth and sucked. Allie's hips bucked. She shoved her hands in his hair as he rubbed his tongue against her before moving to her other breast. The rasp of his tongue, the gentle abrasion of his teeth against her sensitized flesh made her knees wobbly. Her thigh muscles quivered.

He raised his head and, watching her face, skimmed his fingers along the elastic at her waist. She involuntarily sucked in her stomach. Gooseflesh prickled her skin. Inch by inch, he pushed her sweatpants past her hips. Down her legs. When her pants were pooled at her feet, he glanced downward.

He exhaled heavily and hooked one finger under the leg of her red, silky panties. His knuckles rubbed against her skin as he slid his hand up to her hip bone, then down. He brushed at the curls between her legs, and her pelvis jerked.

He reached behind her, shoved aside the skillet he'd put there earlier, and lifted her. She gasped, both from the feel of the cold countertop against her bare thighs and the ease at which he'd set her up there. When she reached for him, he forced her arms back to her sides.

"Hold on to this." His voice was ragged as he pressed her hands against the counter edge. He must've seen her confusion because he shook his head. "I lose control when you touch me."

His admission made her feel sexy. And powerful. "I don't want you to be in control."

"Yes. You do. And so do I," he said, so solemnly, she wrapped her fingers around the counter's edge.

He smiled and her heart picked up speed. He leaned forward and kissed her, kept kissing her while he caressed her breasts. Her body grew warm and relaxed. Still kissing her, he skimmed his hands down her rib cage, over her hips and settled them on her thighs. He pulled back and searched her face as he trailed his fingers across her collarbones, over her shoulders and down her arms.

Her own fingers tightened their grip on the counter. Dean lightly stroked her legs, over her knee to her ankle and back up. He placed one hand on each thigh and nudged them apart.

When she tensed and tried to draw her knees together, he lifted his head. "Trust me," he whispered.

She swallowed. That was the problem. She liked

him. He was steady and solid and one of those guys who loved to ride to the rescue. And she wanted him. Wanted him so much it scared her.

But trust him? How could she when she was too afraid to trust anyone ever again?

None of that mattered now. She needed to forget, just for a little while. To stop worrying. Stop thinking.

All she wanted was to feel.

And Dean seemed more than willing to help with that.

She let her legs fall open. He stepped between them and kissed her once, stroking her hair. He touched her everywhere, his hands caressing her as if he wanted to memorize the shape of her. The feel. From her breasts to her thighs and calves and back again, leaving tingles of sensation in his wake…

Her head fell back against the cabinet as he repeated the process. He took her breast in his mouth again and she squirmed. He pulled her closer so that she sat at the edge of the counter, and then he skimmed his fingers over her panties, between her thighs.

It felt so good. But it wasn't enough.

Dean continued those feathery strokes as he moved to her other breast, his free palm rubbing against the nipple he'd just released. Her mouth opened as she dug her heels into the counter below and thrust against his hand.

But instead of heeding her silent command for him to touch her harder, faster—to tear away her panties and touch her, skin to skin—he continued his slow torture.

He released her breasts and dropped to his knees. "Watch me touch you," he commanded softly.

And he pressed his mouth to her and exhaled, his hot

breath washing over her. The world spun, pressure building slowly, and when he scraped his teeth against her, she cried out as waves of pleasure spiraled through her.

Breathing hard, her entire body a quivering mass, she slid to her feet. But Dean was there to hold her up, his face pressed against her neck, his body taut against hers.

She finally managed to lift her head and brush her hair back. "I'm going to need a quick moment to recover the use of my legs. Or else," she said huskily as she kissed his neck, "you could always carry me up to the bedroom."

He reacted as if she'd taken a big old bite out of him.

She blinked. "You okay?"

He nodded, but didn't look okay. His mouth was tight, his hands clenched at his sides.

She was more than ready to finish what he'd started. But when she reached for him, panic crossed his face.

"I have to go," he blurted.

Her eyes widened. "What? But…why?"

He took two quick steps back. "I just…have to."

Goose bumps covered Allie's skin and she pulled up her pants. Picking up her sweatshirt, she held it in front of her. "Dean, what's going on?"

"Nothing." But he wouldn't look at her. "I'll see you tonight."

Then he left. As fast as he could go.

Persephone padded into the kitchen, sat and tilted her head at Allie.

"Don't look at me," she said, slumping back against the counter. "I'm as surprised as you are."

And while she usually liked surprises, this one just plain sucked. If she hadn't been on the receiving end of his very clear interest, if she hadn't felt his arousal, she'd be having a major case of performance anxiety about now.

She straightened and roughly pulled her shirt on. After a few calming breaths, she picked up her cat. There was definitely more to Dean's quick escape then second thoughts. Something important.

"I have no idea what happened," she said as she scratched behind Persephone's ears. "But you can bet I'm going to find out."

CHAPTER ELEVEN

DEAN DROVE WITH BOTH windows down and the heater off. He pulled into the motel's driveway before his blood cooled off enough for him to think straight. Parking in front of his room, he rolled the windows up.

He slammed his fist against the steering wheel. What was wrong with him? Why hadn't he gotten out of there when she'd lied to him about not seeing Lynne Addison again? He should've hightailed it back to his room, called Nolan and gotten to work trying to link Allie to Lynne and Jon's disappearance.

Instead, he'd given in to his need to comfort her.

And then he'd just given in to his need for her.

There had been nothing contrived or planned in his actions. Hell, he'd even managed to maintain control when she'd kissed him. But then she'd looked up at him, a self-deprecating smile on her beautiful face, and he couldn't stop himself.

He hit the steering wheel again. He *should've* stopped himself.

Who was he kidding? He'd crossed a line. There was right and there was wrong.

The worst part was, he couldn't even regret it. He'd just have to make damn sure it never happened again.

He climbed out of the truck and unlocked the door to his room. After tossing his motel key card and truck keys on the table, he fell face-first onto the bed. And tried not to think about what he was missing by not carrying Allie up to her bedroom.

His cell phone buzzed and he shifted, digging it out of his front pocket. Caller ID showed Nolan's number. Dean flipped his phone open. "Hey. What's up?"

"I've been trying to reach you for the past hour," his partner groused. "What's the use of having a cell phone if you're not going to answer it?"

"I didn't hear it ring," Dean lied, remembering when it had vibrated back at Allie's house. "You need something?"

"I may have found that connection." His excitement meant he believed they were close to a breakthrough. "The one that proves your hunch about Allison Martin is on target."

Dean rolled over and sat up. "What?"

"Lynne and her son were last seen in that high-priced bookstore-café, Montgomery's, right?"

"Right. Lynne bought a couple of books for the kid and paid with her credit card. It was the last credit card transaction she made."

"Remember how we thought it was weird she'd gone to that particular bookstore, since it was six blocks from the park she was taking Jon to? Six blocks in the opposite direction? And that there are no records indicating she'd ever stepped inside Montgomery's before? No receipts. And none of the employees had ever seen her before that day."

"And this proves my theory how?"

"It seems the only clerk working at the time Lynne and Jon were in Montgomery's was Sarah Lambert, a twenty-five-year-old, part-time college student. Now here's where things get interesting." Dean could hear papers rustling as Nolan searched through his notes. "It seems that when Miss Lambert was nineteen, she was charged with voluntary manslaughter for the shooting death of her junkie boyfriend. At the time, Sarah was also an addict, and couldn't afford legal representation, so an up-and-coming attorney in the public defender's office took the case."

Dean stood, his fingers tightening on his phone. "Allison?"

"Bingo. She argued Sarah acted in self-defense, as the boyfriend had a history of abuse. Halfway through the trial, the D.A. offered a deal. Sarah spent a few years in medium security lockup, got clean and earned her high school diploma. I wasn't sure you were right about this," Nolan admitted. "But if we can find a reasonable motive as to why Allison Martin would defend Addison, only to turn around and help his wife and kid run off, we might be able to blow this thing wide open."

Dean viciously kicked his duffel bag across the room. Why did he have to be right? Why couldn't Allie have been clueless about Lynne and Jon's whereabouts?

I knew I had to make things right. That's what Allie had said after she'd told him she'd realized Addison had been guilty. Helping his wife escape was obviously her way of making things right.

But did she know where they were now? Or had she given them enough money to get by, and then left them to their own devices?

He tipped his head back and blew out a breath. He could tell Nolan he hadn't found a motive or a connection that proved Allie had helped Lynne. He might even be able to convince his partner that the information he'd discovered about Sarah Lambert was a coincidence. If Dean kept what he knew to himself, he could leave. Pack up and be gone before he got even more involved with Allie. He could put something else before the job and just…walk away.

After all, from what Allie had told him and from the information they had from Robin, who's to say Allie hadn't been right to help Lynne get away from her husband?

"Hey, you still there?" Nolan asked.

Dean sighed. "Yeah. Sorry. I think we lost the signal for a minute."

Nolan grunted. "I'll be glad when this case is over. I can appreciate Robin wanting to see her daughter and grandson again, but the way she keeps breathing down my neck, it's like she's inside my shirt. Lucky for me, you're the one who's going to have to give her an update Saturday."

"What?"

"She wants to meet with you face-to-face, and since we told her you were following leads in Cincy, you get a chance to play coddle the client."

"Damn it, I don't have time for this, Nolan. Not when I'm finally getting somewhere."

"You're getting somewhere?"

"I found Allie's motive," Dean said slowly. He filled Nolan in on what she had told him. "Her empty bank accounts and the fact that she had to get a loan to buy

The Summit make sense now. I'm guessing she gave money to the Addisons, since they had no way of getting cash on their own."

"I'm on the red-eye to New York tonight," Nolan said. "I'll talk to Sarah, play up how she could be busted for lying to the cops, interfering with an investigation… the works."

Dean's stomach tightened. "Yeah, that's what I'd do, too. If she played a part in helping them disappear, she might get nervous."

"Exactly. And people who are nervous often screw up. Who knows? She might lead us right to Lynne and Jon."

"At the very least, maybe she'll contact Allie. Either way, I'm going to stick close to Allison." He clenched his hand as he remembered just how close he'd been to her not twenty minutes ago.

SATURDAY, Dean paid the cabbie and stepped out into the brisk wind. His brain was turning after a sleepless night and an early morning drive into Syracuse so he could catch the flight to Cincinnati for his 10:00 a.m. meeting with Robin Hawley. And the information he'd discovered about Miles Addison.

Mainly that there had been rumors of Addison abusing boys in both Boston, where he'd lived before moving to New York, and his hometown of Chicago. The cops who investigated told Dean they'd found evidence money had exchanged hands between Miles and the victims' family, but no formal charges were ever filed.

Seemed the prick really had a system down. From

what Dean gathered, Addison targeted underprivileged boys without strong father figures. He earned their trust simply by paying attention to them, taking them places and buying them things.

The detectives Dean spoke with who'd investigated Addison in Boston and Chicago had wanted to take the case to trial. Unfortunately, without the victims' testimony, they didn't have a shot of getting a conviction.

Too bad. If there was someone who deserved to be behind bars, it was Miles Addison.

Dean entered the crowded coffee shop. He couldn't believe he'd let Nolan talk him into meeting Robin Hawley, but as his partner had pointed out, if Dean didn't meet with her, she might call the investigation off.

Dean spotted her at a corner table in the back of the large, noisy room. She looked the same as the day she'd come to their office in Dallas to hire them, tidy as a preacher's wife at Sunday services. Her silver hair was shorter than Dean's, but instead of looking mannish, the style complemented Robin's softly lined features.

She lifted a hand in greeting as he approached, the sleeve of her subdued pink blouse sliding back to reveal a slim, expensive-looking silver watch.

"Thank you for meeting with me," Robin said when Dean reached the table. She gestured to the empty seat across from her. "Can I get you something? Coffee?"

"No, thank you, ma'am," he said as he sat down. "I'm afraid I don't have much time."

"I understand, and I appreciate how dedicated you and Mr. Winchester are to your job."

Her eyes welled with tears and Dean shifted uncomfortably. *Please don't let her start crying.* That was the last thing he needed. This was Nolan's job, not his. Dean was the one who infiltrated people's lives, tracked down leads and sifted through the lies until he found the truth.

He wasn't cut out for customer care.

Robin shook her head. "I'm sorry. I just miss them both so much." She opened her purse and took out some photos, handing them to Dean. "I wasn't sure if you needed more pictures. That one," she said, pointing to the top picture, "was taken a few months before the trial."

Dean glanced down at the picture of Robin and Lynne dressed up in front of some sort of fancy fountain. Both women were holding champagne glasses and smiling.

Dean flipped to the next photo, in which Robin knelt next to Jon, her arm around his shoulders. The boy wearing a backpack that was at least as big as he was, didn't look as thrilled as she did.

"That was Jonny's first day of kindergarten," Robin said, her voice thick with emotion. "I'm not sure who was more nervous, him or Lynne. Once he got to his classroom, he was fine—he's such an easygoing, friendly boy." She laughed sadly. "But poor Lynne was such a wreck. She stood in the hallway for two hours just to make sure he was really all right."

"We're doing everything possible to find your daughter and grandson, Mrs. Hawley," Dean said, tapping the edge of the photos against the table.

She sipped her coffee. "Mr. Winchester said you might have a new lead?"

"We're following up on several possibilities," he told her, trying to make it sound as if he wasn't hedging. He and Nolan had learned early on that while it was important to keep clients informed, too much information in the wrong hands could shoot a case all to hell. "We're positive Lynne and Jon lived right here in Cincinnati until a few months ago."

He then filled her in as much as he could while keeping Allie's possible connection—and his work in Serenity Springs—to himself.

"You've gotten much further than the other three firms I tried," she said, sounding hopeful. "Maybe this time I'll really find them."

"Like I said, we'll do our best."

She sat up straighter in her chair. "That's all I can ask, isn't it? I know you're in a hurry, so I won't keep you any longer, but I just want to reiterate the condition that if you find Lynne, you don't mention my involvement." She tore at her paper napkin. "I need to face her myself and if she finds out I'm looking for her, she may run away again before I apologize. I was so wrong to testify at the trial, but at the time, I honestly thought I was doing the right thing. What Lynne wanted."

"You believed your son-in-law was innocent?"

"Of course. Everyone did, even Lynne."

"What changed your mind?"

Her lips thinned. "Actually, I'm not convinced he was guilty. All I know is that Lynne left him for a reason and didn't feel she could come to me for help. Whether Miles is guilty or not, the end result is the same. My daughter and grandson are out there somewhere and I may never see them again." She swallowed. "I may never get the chance to apologize." Her eyes beseeched him. "All I want is my family back."

He nodded. Yeah, he could relate. He stood and tucked the pictures in his pocket. "I appreciate the photos. We'll be in touch, but if you have any questions, just call Nolan. He's easier to get ahold of than I am," he lied, having no qualms about throwing his best friend under the bus.

Dean made his way back to the door, thinking about the similarities between what had happened with him and his family and Robin and her daughter. Once outside, he went to the curb to hail a cab back to the airport. His family crap wasn't important. What mattered was getting this job done. If they didn't, Robin would hire someone else, that much was a given. And if she did, that other PI might discover Allie's involvement with the case. She could be accused of aiding and abetting a child abduction

No. This was Dean's job. He'd find Lynne, reunite her with her mother and help Allie get rid of the guilt she'd been carrying around these past two years.

He'd help her get on with her life.

Once she realizes I'm not going to force Lynne to go back to her bastard of a husband, Allie might even be grateful to have my help.

If she ever forgave him for lying to her.

ALLIE HAD NEVER HAD A MAN ignore her for three days before.

Actually, she'd never had a man ignore her for as much as three minutes. She couldn't say she liked it.

She smiled distractedly at the two couples she'd just taken drink orders from, and lifted her full tray. She wove her way back through the crowd. Kelsey's Speed Date Your Way Through Valentine's Day was a hit. The Summit had been packed since the event started at eight, and though there were only two ten-minute sessions left, it didn't look as if the event was losing any steam.

She went behind the bar and set the tray down. Noreen was picking up empty glasses and bottles by the pool table, while Kelsey worked the right side. Since this was Kelsey's baby, Allie had left her in charge of all the setup logistics, keeping time for the dates and planning the mix-and-mingle periods.

She glanced at Dean, who was filling drink orders at the other end of the bar.

She just didn't get it. Ever since he'd left her house Thursday morning, he'd managed to pretend she didn't exist. She tossed an empty into the recycling bin with a loud clang. He'd speak to her if she asked him a direct question, but he didn't meet her eye. And as soon as he'd answered her, he'd find some task that needed his immediate attention.

The way he was acting, you'd think he'd been the one left standing practically naked in the kitchen.

"Would you stop?" Kelsey asked as she came up beside her.

Allie looked away from Dean's strong profile and frowned. "Stop what?"

Her sister-in-law added a shot of rum to a glass and then topped it off with cola. "Stop mooning over your bartender. It's pathetic, so knock it off."

Allie's jaw dropped. "Excuse me," she said haughtily, "but I've never mooned over a man in my life."

"You've never *had* to moon over a man before." Kelsey stuck a stir straw in the glass and gave Allie a knowing look. "Most guys go gaga over you and generally make asses of themselves trying to get you to notice them. So even though I wish you'd set your sights somewhere else, I'm glad he's smart enough not to give you the time of day."

Allie narrowed her eyes as Kelsey handed the drink to a customer. When she came back from ringing up the sale and taking another order, Allie said, "You're supposed to be on my side. And I haven't set my sights on Dean." She lowered her voice. "We had a…moment the other day—"

"Crap," Kelsey said, opening a bottle of beer and setting it on the bar. "You slept with him."

The guy waiting for his drinks grinned. Allie's face heated.

"I did not sleep with him," she hissed, turning her back to the bar. "I'm just wondering what's going on with him."

Kelsey opened another beer and, after the customer left, pulled Allie to the back of the bar. "You want to know why he's ignoring you after your shared moment—in which no sex was involved. Is that about right?"

"I want to make sure he's okay, that's all. He's been acting strangely and—"

"You only met the guy a week ago," Kelsey said. "How do you know if he's acting strangely or not?"

"I just know."

"Why must I do everything?" Kelsey muttered to no

one in particular. Then she strode toward Dean. Not liking the look in her eyes, Allie followed. When Kelsey glanced back at her, she turned and stuck her hands in the sink, as if her intention all along had been to wash dishes.

"How's it going?" Kelsey asked him.

He didn't even look up from the beer he was pouring. "Other than that damn air horn blasting every ten minutes and a line five deep because you chat more than you pour drinks, it's going great."

"Hey, that air horn is the cue for people to move on to the next date. And there are only two left, so you'll just have to deal. And I wouldn't have to stop and chat if you hadn't had a *moment* with your boss the other day and are now determined to ignore her."

He gaped at Allie, his hand still on the beer tap. "You told her?"

She clenched her teeth. What did he think, that she'd told Kelsey he'd given her a mind-blowing orgasm in the middle of her kitchen?

"I didn't tell her anything because there was nothing to tell," Allie stated. She nodded at the overflowing glass in his hand. "And you're wasting beer."

He looked down and cursed. Turning off the tap, he carried the beer to his waiting customer.

"And just for the record," she said to her sister-in-law, rinsing a glass, "I don't appreciate you sticking your nose where it doesn't belong."

"I was only trying to help." Kelsey tried but failed to pull off an innocent expression. "I butt in because I care."

Allie knew that. But it didn't make her any less angry. "Well, I'll handle things from here." She pointed a wet finger to the lineup of thirsty people. "Now would you please get back to work before you force me to fire your skinny ass?"

"Killjoy." Kelsey pouted.

Within fifteen minutes, another ten-minute dating session had started and the line had died down enough for Allie to have cleaned most of the glasses. She'd had enough time to think a few things through. The other day Dean had asked her when she was going to stop allowing her fear of making another mistake rule her actions. She hadn't realized until this moment exactly how much she'd changed. If a man had run off on her two years ago, she would've tracked him down and demanded an explanation. But now, all she did was wait around like some timid schoolgirl with her first crush.

Somewhere along the line, she'd lost her faith in herself. And she wanted it back.

She waited until Dean had a break, then told Kelsey to cover the bar before following him into the kitchen. "You've been avoiding me," she said, as she entered the room.

"I haven't been—"

"Bull. I know why you're doing it, just as I know why you walked away from me the other day."

He seemed leery, as if she'd guessed some big, dark secret. "You do?"

She nodded. "You didn't want to take advantage of me. Which is sweet—" His laughter cut her off. She frowned. "What?"

"Oh, I wanted to take advantage," he said with a sexy grin. "Believe me."

She cleared her throat. "Well, be that as it may, you didn't. Uh, take advantage of my…weak moment. And I want you to know, since I wasn't thinking clearly at the time, I appreciate your restraint and good judgment."

He turned the water bottle in his hands. "So you're glad we didn't go any further?"

Hell, no. "Yes. I am. Just because we're…attracted…to each other doesn't mean we can't control our baser instincts. We're not animals."

"Speak for yourself," he mumbled.

"Excuse me?"

"Nothing."

"So we're both in agreement that nothing…irreversible happened between us. There's no reason for you to avoid me. We can get back to being what we were before…"

"You mean, boss and employer?"

"Yes, but I think we can be more than that. Friends."

He seemed less than thrilled by the idea. "Don't you have enough of those?"

"There's always room for one more," she told him with a wink. Then she walked away. And for the first time since she'd moved back to Serenity Springs, she felt like her old self.

CHAPTER TWELVE

HALF AN HOUR LATER the speed dating thing had ended—and Dean had tossed the air horn in the Dumpster out back. He mixed what had to be his sixtieth cosmopolitan of the night and wondered about the allure of pink drinks. The ladies in The Summit sure couldn't get enough of them.

Probably because Allie had made all red and pink drinks half price in honor of Valentine's Day.

After finishing the order, he dunked a fresh cloth in cleaning solution. He heard the unmistakable sound of Allie's laughter, which was crazy seeing as the noise level in the room was off the charts. Wringing out the cloth, he raised his head as he searched the crowd for her.

He slapped the cloth onto the counter when he found her holding court by the pool table with a half dozen males of various shape, size and age. The only thing they had in common was their open appreciation of Allie.

Or at least, their appreciation of how well she filled out that damn red sweater of hers.

Dean scrubbed at the counter. He hadn't been able to stop thinking about what happened in her kitchen the other day. How she'd felt under his hands and mouth. How she'd trembled.

"I take it you're not into competition?" Kelsey sidled up next to him, a smirk on her face.

"Why?" he asked. "You want to challenge me to an arm wrestling match?"

"If I thought I could win, you bet." She nodded toward the small jungle of flowers by the cash register. "How many bouquets do you think Allie got today? Five? Six?"

"Eight," he said before he could stop himself.

She pursed her lips. "Right. Eight. Plus three boxes of candy and one very ugly red teddy bear. What does that tell you?"

"That the florists and gift shops in Serenity Springs praise the day she moved back to town?"

Kelsey opened a bottle of water and took a long drink, watching him steadily over the rim. "You know, despite my initial doubts, I think I could learn to like you."

"I'm a very likable guy." He gave her his most charming grin.

She twisted the cap back on the bottle. Untwisted it. "Be that as it may, I can't help but wonder if you're pulling the deep freeze on Allie because of all the attention she gets from the opposite sex." She gave his hand a pat. "What's the matter? Feeling insecure?"

"I'm not freezing her out and I'm not threatened by the attention she gets from, or gives to, the opposite sex. Allie and I have a business relationship. Period."

"For your sake, I hope you're telling the truth. Because if you do anything to hurt her," Kelsey said, pointing her bottle at him like a weapon, "I will come after you like the wrath of God."

He'd been warned off by a redhead who probably weighed one hundred and ten pounds soaking wet. And yet he was just the slightest bit scared of her.

One thing was for sure. This job hadn't been boring.

He watched Allie lead a middle-aged man in a dark suit over to a back table. "You don't think she can take care of herself?"

"Please. Allie can take care of herself, this bar and half the population of Serenity Springs without breaking one perfectly manicured nail."

"Exactly." Dean gestured to a chubby brunette, one of the many women who'd come for the speed dating, that he'd be with her in a moment. He turned back to Kelsey. "Allie's one of the smartest, savviest, most capable people I've ever met. But if it'll set your mind at ease—and get you off my back—I promise I'll do everything in my power not to hurt her."

He left Kelsey with a thoughtful frown on her face.

"Evening," he said to the brunette. "What can I get you?"

Behind her black, rectangular glasses, she blinked her muddy-brown eyes. "Uh…white wine?"

He grinned. "You asking or ordering?"

She brushed her heavy, brow skimming bangs to the side. "Sorry. I'd like a glass of white wine. Chardon-nay, please."

She took off her gray coat and then dug through her purse as he poured. While he knew she hadn't been in The Summit before, he must've seen her around town because she seemed vaguely familiar. Then again, during the course of the evening he'd recognized several Serenity Springs's singles taking part in the speed dating, including a bubbly redhead who worked at the bakery, a local cop who looked more like a linebacker, and the guy who delivered mail to the bar.

The woman pulled out her cell phone and a twenty and set her bag aside. Twisting a chunk of drab brown, shoulder-length hair around her finger as she opened her phone, she checked something, then closed it again.

"Here you go." He set her drink in front of her.

"Thank you." She handed him the twenty but knocked her glass over. "Oh!" She grabbed her phone with one hand, righted the now empty glass with the other. "I'm so sorry. I'm such a klutz."

"No problem." Dean wiped up the mess and took the glass from her. "Let me get you another one. On the house."

She blushed and shook her head. "Thank you, but I'd rather pay for both."

"It's really not—"

"I insist."

He raised his eyebrows. Who knew a stubborn streak could be hidden under such a plain exterior? Guess that proved what his mother always said about not judging by appearances. Was his mom ever wrong?

He refilled the customer's glass. "Can I get you anything else?"

She smiled shyly at him. "No, thanks."

He rang up her wine—both glasses—and handed her the change. "You here for the dating extravaganza?" he asked, even though he'd seen her switching dates a few times this evening.

She sipped her wine. "My boss asked me to come with her, and I've always had a hard time saying no to the person signing my paycheck."

He nodded at the college kid who held up his empty glass. Mixing another rum and coke, Dean realized where he'd seen her before. She worked at that beauty parlor next to the pizza place on Union Street. He'd followed Allie there on Wednesday and seen the brunette through the window.

He gave the rum and coke to his customer as Allie joined them. "Ellen," she said as she hugged the brunette. "I didn't know you were coming tonight."

"Georgie talked me into it. She didn't want to come alone so…"

"So you got stuck playing her wing-woman?"

Ellen smiled. "She's been so good to me, I didn't see the harm."

"So, how was it?" Allie asked. "Did you meet anyone special? Make plans to get together again?"

Ellen looked as horrified as if Allie had just attempted to pimp her out to the highest bidder. "No. I mean… I wasn't serious. It was more to pass the time."

"Well, that's too bad," Allie said. "I saw you sitting with Jared during that last round and he's so nice—cute and smart *and* funny. The kids he teaches at the high school love him. If you want I could—"

"Hey, Yentl," Dean said to Allie when he noticed Ellen's pale face and the death grip she had on her purse, "ease up on the hard sell."

Allie glared at him before she saw how freaked out Ellen was. "Sorry. I guess I…got carried away by the spirit of the evening."

"I appreciate the offer but really, I'm not interested."

"No problem. If you change your mind, though, Jared is a very nice man."

Dean winced. Sweet God, if a woman as sexy as Allie ever described him as a very nice man in any context whatsoever, he hoped someone would shoot him and end his misery.

He waited on another customer while Allie and Ellen chatted. When he returned, the brunette was gone.

"What happened?" he asked Allie. "Did you scare her off?"

"Hardly." She scooped ice into a glass and poured cranberry juice over it. "Her son's recovering from a bad cold so she went home."

"More than likely she got out of here before you brought up nice-guy Jared again."

"It's not like I dragged the man over here," she said, waving the bar's soda gun around. "I was simply pointing out that if she was in the market for a date, so to speak, she could do a lot worse than Jared." Allie stabbed a straw into her glass. "I didn't sell her into matrimony."

"I thought after what happened with Richie you were going to stop saving the world and put yourself first?"

She met his eyes. "I tried that the other day. It didn't quite work out, remember?"

His phone vibrated, but even though he was waiting for a call from Nolan, Dean ignored it. He edged closer.

He was so tired of keeping his distance, of fighting his feelings for Allie. She stood her ground.

"Seems to me things worked out just fine for you that morning," he said huskily. He slid a finger over the back of her hand. "And I sure don't have any complaints."

Instead of backing up as he expected her to do, she took a step forward so that their thighs brushed. "If you hadn't run off, you wouldn't have had any complaints about what happened next, either."

His mind blanked and then filled with images of them together. "You might not understand this," he told her, "but I'm trying to do the right thing here."

Her smile was slow and sensual. "Who's stopping you? Now, you might want to answer your phone or turn it off. Or else people are going to think that vibrating bulge in your pocket is something else entirely."

"Hello?" Luckily, the voice on the other end wasn't Nolan's, or else in Dean's state, he'd probably blow his cover wide open.

"Hello, sugar! Happy Valentine's Day."

Even though it'd been this past Christmas since he'd last heard that voice, he had no trouble placing it. "Mama?" He noticed Allie watching him curiously. "Is everything all right?"

"Everything's just fine, thanks in part to the gorgeous dozen roses you sent. But a visit from you in person would've been even better."

There was no way he could fend off his mother's reproach while under his boss's watchful eyes. "Could you hold on a minute?" He covered the mouthpiece. "Do you mind if I take a quick break?" he asked Allie.

"By all means," she said, shooing him away. "I'll handle your end of the bar."

He nodded and brought the phone back up to his ear, holding his free hand over his other ear to block out some of the noise. One good thing about talking to his mother, hearing her voice killed any sexual thoughts he might have been having about Allie.

He might have to send her another dozen roses just for that.

ALLIE PULLED TWO DRAFTS and had Kelsey mix up a raspberry lemon drop, which she gave the customer for half price as part of her Valentine's Day red drink promotion. Allie was pouring three shots of Jack Daniel's for a trio of twenty-something guys in jeans and polos when Dean returned.

"Thanks," he said, filling the next order for an imported beer. "I'll take it from here."

"This the no-good, untrustworthy, womanizing cowboy I've been hearing way too much about?"

Next to her, Dean bristled. Allie sighed. "Did Kelsey really call him a womanizer or did you make that part up?" she asked Dillon Ward, who stood at the bar, his arm around Nina Carlson's waist.

Dillon ran his free hand through his auburn hair. Even though she could tell he'd recently had a trim, the ends still reached his collar. "You think I would use the word *womanizer* on my own?"

"Well, in that case, yes, this is him," Allie said. "Dean, these are dear friends of mine, Dillon Ward and Nina Carlson. Dillon is Kelsey's brother."

"That would explain it," Dean said.

"Nice to meet you." Nina's dimple flashed as she smiled. She turned to Dillon. "While you two do your manly, sizing each other up thing, I'm going to go over and say hi to Kelsey." She kissed his cheek, rolled her eyes at Allie and walked away.

"I have customers waiting," Dean said. "I think I'll skip the sizing up portion of the evening."

Watching Dean move down to serve the next person, Allie leaned her elbows on the bar. "Good to see you still know how to clear a room with your sparkling personality, Dillon."

"Room's still full. I want to talk to you."

"If you're here to discuss Dean—"

"The cowboy?" He laughed. "I'm not. We both know that if you wanted, you could have him wrapped around your little finger. My sister's time would be better spent worrying about how that poor bastard's going to survive *you*."

"It's not like that between me and—oh, sit down." She opened a bottle of his favorite beer and gestured toward an empty stool.

He shoved his hands into his coat pockets. "Can we go into the kitchen? I need to ask you something."

"Sure." She took his beer and her drink, told Kelsey she'd be right back, and followed him out of the room. "What's up?" she asked as she sat at the table. "Is everything okay with Nina and the kids?"

"Yeah, they're all fine." But he wouldn't look at her and he kept pacing.

"Trey didn't get his visitation rights back, did he?"

A few months ago, Nina had petitioned family court to grant her full custody of her two young children. She had needed to get them away from her ex-husband's physical and emotional abuse.

"No, he still only has supervised visits twice a week for a few hours."

She wiped her damp palms down the legs of her jeans. "Well, what is it then?"

Dillon dug into his pocket, pulled out a silver jeweler's box and slammed it onto the table. "Open it."

Her heart racing, Allie set her drink aside before lifting the lid. "Oh," she breathed, "it's beautiful." She held the box up so the solitary princess diamond caught the light. She glanced at him. "But shouldn't you be kneeling? If a guy's going to propose to me, he'd better want me badly enough to get on his knee."

"Then it's lucky for me I'm not proposing to you, isn't it?"

"That's a shame, because to get my hands on this ring—or should I say, to get this ring on my hand—I might have said yes."

He snatched the box from her, scowling. "Do you think Nina will like it?"

Allie stood and squeezed his arm. "If she doesn't, she's not the woman I think she is."

He snapped the lid shut. "It's not much. The ring Trey gave her was probably bigger. Flashier."

"Are you kidding?" Allie's heart was so full of love for him, she thought it would burst. "That sucker was huge. It was like she had a small boulder on her finger."

He gave her one of his I'm-a-big-bad-ex-convict-

and-you'd-better-not-mess-with-me looks. The one that had sent more than one person in town running.

"Don't be an idiot. This ring is perfect. Besides, do you really think Nina's going to care about what size diamond you give her? Or worse, compare you to Trey?"

He tapped the box against his thigh. "You're right. It's just that... I'm so nervous. I haven't been this afraid since my first day in prison," he admitted quietly.

"Any time a man asks a woman to marry him, he should be nervous." Allie rubbed his back. "But Nina's crazy about you. And so are her kids."

He stuck the box back in his pocket. "The feeling's mutual." He took a long drink from his beer, leaning against the table, then he picked at the label on the bottle. "I even got Hayley a necklace with a diamond that matches the ring. I wasn't sure what to give Marcus so I wrote him a letter, telling him how proud I am of him and how I'll always be there for him no matter what."

Her eyes welled. How could such a strong man seem so unsure of himself because he wanted to make the people he loved happy? Because he wanted to do right by them?

"The necklace and the letter are both wonderful, thoughtful gifts," she said. "Nina and the kids are so lucky to have you in their lives."

"Hey," he said, straightening quickly and setting down his beer, "turn off the waterworks. You'd think someone died or something."

She sniffed but couldn't stop the tears from running down her face. "I'm so happy for you. Less than a year ago you were pathetic and alone—"

"Pathetic?" He looked to the ceiling. "Why me?"

"I was your only friend—"

"What you were was a pain in the ass who wouldn't let me live in peace."

"No one would hire you. Half the town was afraid of you." She crossed to the counter for a paper towel. Wiped her nose. "And you spent most of your time cultivating your dangerous reputation so people wouldn't find out that underneath that tough-guy exterior is nothing but a big old mushy teddy bear."

He pinched the bridge of his nose. "If you don't knock it off, I might start bawling, too."

"And now you have a relationship with your sister again and you're in love with a wonderful woman— a woman who loves you right back and whose kids are nuts over you," Allie said, her voice breaking. "I'm ju-just...so ec-ecstat...happy for you!" She jumped into his arms, sobbing into his neck. "You deserve a family of your own." She leaned back and grinned, her face still wet with tears. "I love you, you know that?"

He rolled his eyes. "Yeah. I know." Then he shocked her by squeezing her tight, which only succeeded in making her cry again in earnest. "I love you, too." He set her on her feet and tapped the end of her nose. "But you're still a pain in the ass."

SHE WAS DRIVING HIM CRAZY.

Dean gritted his teeth and slammed a chair onto a table. He could ignore Allie playing the radio, filling the empty bar with the latest pop tunes instead of the classic rock on the jukebox. He could even deal with her singing along to aforementioned pop songs, mostly because, as he'd noticed when he'd walked into the kitchen for his interview last week, she didn't sound half-bad.

But he couldn't handle how she shimmied and otherwise shook her ass to each and every song. Or worse, the stab of jealousy he'd felt earlier when she'd walked out of the kitchen with Dillon Ward, her arm linked with his, her head on his shoulder. Tears in her eyes.

Wondering what she'd been crying about—and why she'd chosen some other man to comfort her instead of him—about killed Dean.

The song slowed and Allie, cloth in hand, straightened from the table she was washing. She closed her eyes and lifted her arms over her head and swayed to the music. He caught his breath, his body tense.

He was too old for this kind of torture. He slammed another chair down.

Her eyes flew open and she frowned, but at least she stopped moving. "You okay?"

"Dandy," he muttered.

"You sure?" She flipped off the radio. "You've been quiet ever since we closed."

"I'm trying to get this done," he said pointedly, "so we can get to bed." Not what he'd meant to say. "So we can get *home*," he amended. "It's been a long day."

Made even longer thanks to Nolan's text message a few hours ago. He hadn't had any luck tracking down Sarah Lambert yet.

"Is everything okay with your mom?" Allie asked.

"What?"

"I couldn't help but overhear you talking with her,"

she said. "It was kind of late for her to be calling, and you've been so grumpy—"

"I am not grumpy," he snapped. She made him sound like a cartoon bear or something.

"I thought…maybe something had happened."

"I said everything's fine."

"Sorry I asked," Allie said going back to wiping off tables, her movements jerky.

Dean sighed. He'd hoped Nolan would have found Sarah by now and gotten the evidence they required to confront Allie about helping Lynne and Jon escape Miles Addison. Dean needed a way to back her into a corner so she'd be forced to tell him the truth. He needed proof.

Without it, he'd be revealing his hand too soon. And he'd lose any headway he'd made in getting Allie to trust him, without anything to show for it.

Dean finished setting the chairs up and went to get the broom.

"Let's leave the floor until tomorrow," Allie said as she stepped behind the bar and washed her hands.

"You sure?"

"You're right, it's been a long day." She opened a heart-shaped box of chocolates, nibbling her lower lip as she chose one. She bit into it, her eyes closing in pleasure.

This job couldn't be over soon enough.

"Want some?" she asked, and damn if her voice didn't sound husky and alluring.

"No, thanks." When she shrugged and chose another chocolate, a growl rose in his throat. "You about ready to go?"

She looked up, no doubt startled at his gruff tone.

"Uh...sure." She put the lid back on the chocolates and stacked it with the other two boxes before picking up a pen. "Let me get the cards off of these flowers first."

"You're not going to take them home?"

"Just the ones from my dad," she said, pointing to a bouquet of yellow roses. She wrote something on the card from one of the three vases of long-stemmed red roses. "The other ones I'll drop off at the hospital tomorrow."

"So all those poor saps who sent you flowers wasted their time and money?"

She narrowed her eyes. "Well, I was going to sleep with them all—one at a time, of course—as a thank-you for them breaking out their credit cards," she said coolly. "Considering I've met most of them only once or twice, that seems beyond generous on my part. But since that would take up my next two months of Saturdays, I decided to draw a name to see which lucky guy got me."

"I didn't mean—"

"On second thought," she said, "I think I'll stay a little while longer. Don't wait for me. I can find my car by myself."

And with that, she lowered her head and gave all her attention to a second florist card.

In the kitchen, he got his coat and carried it back out. She didn't look up when he stood in front of her, separated by the bar.

"I didn't get you flowers," he said, as if challenging her to make a big deal of it.

She slowly lifted her head and tucked her hair behind her ear. "I didn't expect you to."

He reached into his pocket and tossed a plastic

grocery bag on top of the card she was writing on. "That's for you."

She nudged the bag with the tip of her pen. "What is it?"

"Just open it."

She unfolded the bag and attempted to smooth out the wrinkles before she gingerly complied. It took all he had not to rip it away from her and dump out the contents. She probably took forever to unwrap her Christmas gifts, too.

She pulled out a small blue bag of trail mix and stared at him.

He scratched the back of his neck. "It has dried cranberries in it, and since you're always drinking cranberry juice, I thought you'd like it."

"I…I do. Thank you."

Then she took out the pink, heart-shaped stuffed mouse.

He twisted his coat in his hands. "I thought maybe Persephone might like it," he said defiantly.

He felt like a fool standing there, a blush heating his neck even as he hoped she liked a bunch of stupid things he'd picked up at the convenience store.

"Dean," she asked, running a finger over the mouse's ears, "what are these? Why are you giving them to me?" Her lips twitched. "Are these Valentine gifts?"

"It's not Valentine's Day anymore."

"So you don't want me to be your valentine?"

He shoved a hand through his hair. "What are we, ten years old?"

"Well, in that case, thank you for the gifts—which you gave me for no particular reason." She put them back in the plastic bag and came around the bar. "But for the record, if you had sent flowers, I'd have taken them home with me."

He cleared his throat. "Give me your keys. I'll warm your car while you finish up."

"Thank you."

"I'm going out to start my truck anyway—"

"No. Thank you for the gifts." She left the room and came back almost immediately with her keys, but instead of handing them over, she clasped them in her hand. "Dean, why did your mother call you tonight?"

"Does she need a reason to call me?"

"So she called to wish you a Happy Valentine's Day?" Too bad his evasive maneuvers didn't fool Allie.

He met her eyes and knew she suspected the real reason for that phone call. How could she know him so well? And why did the thought scare him so much?

"She called to thank me for the flowers I sent her. And," he admitted, "to tell me that Rene loved the carnations and balloons I sent her."

"Rene?"

"My niece."

Allie smiled. "You sent your niece flowers?" she asked, as if he'd single-handedly stopped global warming. "Did you talk to your brother? If you want to go down to Dallas, I'm sure we could figure a way to give you a couple of days off."

"I didn't talk to Ryan or Jolene, and I don't think any of us are ready for me to pop up on their doorstep." Allie looked so disappointed Dean almost grinned. She sure was a sweetheart. "I'm taking things one step at a time."

Steps he should've taken years ago, he knew. Steps he hadn't been able to take until he'd opened up to Allie about the loss of his son. That, combined with witnessing Robin Hawley's need for forgiveness from her daughter, made Dean realize he had to stop being a coward and make amends.

She nodded. "I know it wasn't easy—"

"All I did was call up a florist and order some flowers. Don't make more of this than it is."

"I'll make more of it if I want to. Just like I'll tell you I'm proud of you if I want to." Before he could evade her, she closed the distance between them, stretched up on her toes and kissed him, a soft, warm press of her lips against his. "You're one of the good guys, Dean."

She couldn't be more wrong.

"Your keys?" he asked.

"Oh. Sure. Sorry." She dropped them into his open palm, confusion on her face. "I'll just be a few more minutes."

He nodded and slipped on his coat. Once outside, he tilted his head back and inhaled deeply, the cold air burning his lungs. He needed to stop straddling the fence with Allie. He needed to tell her what he was really doing there.

He just hoped like hell she'd forgive him.

Maybe she'd understand. After all, he wanted to reunite Lynne and Jon Addison with Robin, not hurt anyone.

Not that it mattered. He couldn't keep this up. He couldn't keep lying to her.

He turned back to the door, but the sound of crunching snow to his left made him stop. He listened, the hair on the back of his neck standing on end. One heartbeat. Two. When he didn't hear anything else, he began to push the door open. Out of the corner of his eye, he saw a shadow. He turned, but it was too late. Pain exploded in the side of his head and he fell face-first into the snow.

CHAPTER THIRTEEN

ALLIE TUCKED THE florist cards in her purse. Even though she didn't want the flowers—or any of the guys who'd sent them—she'd still acknowledge the gifts from the men she personally knew. Of course, she'd already thanked the two guys who'd delivered their own gifts. And let them know, as politely as possible, she wasn't interested. Despite what Dean thought about her flirting, she had a strict policy about not leading men on.

She'd keep the three boxes of chocolates, though.

She put her coat on and pulled her hair out from under the collar before picking up the flowers from her dad.

She heard the door open. "Just in time." She turned and almost dropped her flowers. "Richie? What are you—"

"You weren't supposed to be here." Her former assistant slammed the door shut.

Her stomach pitched. His hair was greasy, his coat open to reveal he had on the same clothes he'd worn the last time she'd seen him. And from the wrinkles and stains, it was clear he hadn't washed them—or himself—since then.

"It's after four," he said, as if she had no right to be in her own bar. "Why are you still here?"

She smiled shakily, trying not to let him see how

uneasy she felt. "Dillon and Nina stopped by," she explained slowly. "They'd taken the kids to a movie and then went out to dinner, so they didn't get here until late. We didn't start cleaning until almost three." She casually put the flowers down and walked out from behind the bar. "I'm so glad you came back…."

It wasn't until she was a few feet away from him that she noticed his dilated pupils. The sweat beaded on his upper lip. The rank scent of body odor.

And the gun held loosely at his side.

The blood drained from her face. "Wha-what are you doing with that?" Her eyes widened and nausea churned her stomach. She stepped toward the door. "Where's Dean?"

"Don't move!" Richie lifted the gun, pointing it at her chest, his hand shaking. "He wasn't supposed to be here, either."

She held her arms out at her sides. "I'm not going to hurt you."

Which was a really ridiculous thing to say, since she wasn't the one with the gun.

And the way he was waving it around didn't bode well for her. He might accidentally shoot her…. Because surely he wouldn't shoot her on purpose.

The Richie she knew, the Richie she'd shared the secret to her rue sauce with, who'd dressed up as Fred Flintstone to her Wilma last Halloween, would never hurt her.

But this wasn't that man, was it? This Richie was strung out, highly agitated and worse, unpredictable. The old Richie was still in there, though. He had to be. All she had to do was get through to him.

"Where's Dean?" she asked again, keeping her voice even. She inched toward the door. "Is he all right?"

Richie wiped the back of his hand over his forehead. "I didn't want to hurt him. I didn't mean for anyone to get hurt."

Her lungs constricted with fear. *Oh, God. No.* "Where is he?"

"Outside. By the door."

Dean had to be all right. If Richie had fired his gun—had shot Dean—she would've heard the discharge. "I need to check on him."

"You can't leave," he said, pointing the gun at her head. "You can't go to the cops."

She swallowed, but the lump in her throat remained. "I'm not leaving. I promise. I'm just going to check on Dean. That's all. Please," she begged. "Let me open the door."

He nodded and slowly lowered the gun, but he didn't put it away. She took a deep breath and prayed she wouldn't find Dean's lifeless body in the parking lot.

Wiping her sweating palms down the front of her jeans, she opened the door. Light spilled out, illuminating Dean's crumpled figure on the sidewalk.

She gasped and raced outside, sliding in her high-heeled boots. Falling to her knees beside him, she frantically felt the side of his neck for a pulse. His skin was cold, his lips tinged blue, but his heartbeat was steady. *Thank you, God.*

"Is he…dead?" Richie asked from the doorway.

"He's breathing." She gently brushed his hair back.

Dots of blood stained the snow from the nasty cut on his temple. He hadn't lost much blood, but he had what promised to become a sizable, and from the looks of it, painful lump.

Dean's eyelids fluttered and he groaned.

"What's he doing?" Richie asked, panicked.

She held Dean's hands, trying to warm them with her own. "Dean? Can you hear me?"

He blinked slowly several times, finally bringing his eyes into focus. She sat back, relieved.

"You all right?" he asked in a low whisper.

Her laugh sounded suspiciously close to a sob. "I'm fine," she said. "You're the one lying in the snow with a head wound."

He raised his hand and gingerly felt the area around the bump. Grimaced. "Just a scratch," he mumbled.

She braced her arm around his shoulder and helped him sit up. "Any dizziness?"

"Nah." But he spoke through gritted teeth as if fighting back a rush of pain.

"What are you doing?" Richie asked.

She didn't even look at him. "I'm helping him get up."

"No. You've seen he's all right, just leave him."

She bit back the urge to snap at him. "We can't leave him out here in the cold," she said, proud of how rational she sounded. As if she was held at gunpoint every day by someone she used to consider a friend. "He's hurt. He could die."

She could've sworn she saw Dean roll his eyes before he winced. Okay, so he probably wouldn't die, but Richie didn't seem to know that.

Richie was now shivering violently—either from drugs or the cold or both. "F-f-fine. But don't t-t-try to run."

"Can you stand?" she asked Dean.

"Yeah."

She put his arm around her shoulder, shifted onto her heels and helped him get to his feet. Staggering under his weight, she somehow managed to keep her balance. He leaned heavily on her as they shuffled inside. Richie walked backward, kept his gun trained on them. As soon as they were in, he shut and locked the door.

"He can sit over there," the young man said, gesturing toward the far corner of the room. The corner farthest away from any of the exits.

Seemed Richie wasn't all that far gone.

"Can you stand on your own for a minute?" Allie asked when they reached the table.

Dean's face was pale, etched with pain. He nodded, but then hissed out a breath as he shifted, a movement that must've hurt like hell. She let go of him and quickly set a chair down, then helped him sink into it.

"That's good," Richie called from the other side of the pool table. "Now…come over here."

Terrified, she forced herself to straighten. She had to let him think he was in control, find a way to talk him down before he did something he'd regret.

She had to believe he wouldn't hurt her or Dean more than he already had.

She took a step, but Dean seized her wrist, his grip surprisingly strong. Startled, she met his eyes.

"Wait for my cue," he said almost soundlessly.

Her mind blanked. What was he saying? What did he mean?

"No talking!" Richie shrieked.

She spun back around, her mouth bone dry. Richie was obviously close to the breaking point. Then the realization hit her and her knees threatened to buckle— Dean wasn't as hurt as he'd made them believe. Make that he wasn't as hurt as he wanted Richie to believe.

"He's thirsty," Allie lied, cursing herself when her voice cracked. "Can I get him some water?"

Richie viciously scratched his neck with his free hand. "No. Just—just get away from him. Come over here."

She hesitated, glanced back at Dean and nodded slightly to let him know she'd heard him before.

"Now!"

Her heart thumping madly, she had to walk away from Dean. Toward Richie.

Everything would be okay. They'd get out of this. All she had to do was keep control of the situation so that no one got hurt.

And if she could, help Richie before it was too late.

"Get the key to the cash register," he told her.

"You…you're going to rob me?" Even though she knew that had been his intention, hearing his demand still came as a shock. "Do you know what the penalty is for armed robbery? At least ten years in a state prison."

She needed to stop him.

He looked at her as if she'd lost her mind. A distinct possibility, considering she was arguing with a man pointing a gun at her.

"Just get the key!" he shouted, spittle flying from his lips, his face red.

Her legs shaking, she went behind the bar, knelt down and pulled the key from the magnet she kept under the sink. Before she stood, she said a quick prayer that whatever Dean was planning, he'd make his move soon.

"Come on, get up." Richie jerked her to her feet, his fingers biting into her arm. She gasped at the pain. "Open the damn cash register."

Her hands were so unsteady, it took her three tries to fit the key in the lock. The drawer sprang open and he nudged her aside. He tensed, then threw the empty money tray over the bar with a curse.

He turned to her and she took a step back, her hand going to her chest. "Where's the money?" he asked.

"I already put it in the safe." She edged to one side, forcing Richie to turn his back on Dean if he was going to keep her in his line of vision. "You know I don't leave that much cash in the register overnight."

He pressed his hands against his temples. "No, no, no." He focused on Dean, who was bent over, his elbows on his thighs, his head resting in his hands. "We'll... we'll tie him up. Then we'll go back to the safe, get the money."

"We can't tie him up," she said, drawing Richie's attention back to her. "There's no rope here."

He looked around frantically. "We'll use something else."

"Like what? There's nothing here."

"I don't know!" He picked up the heavy glass mixer and heaved it toward the shelves of liquor. She covered her head as bottles exploded, sending shards of glass flying through the air, stinging the back of her hands. The distinctive smell of liquor filled the room.

Richie was breathing hard, but she didn't dare look to see what Dean was doing. Not if she wanted to keep Richie's attention on her. "You need to stay calm—"

"Shut up!" He pointed the gun at her. "Shut up. I— I need to think. I need—"

"You don't have to do this," she told him, fighting the fear clawing her throat. "It's not too late to end this right now. Before it gets worse. Before you do something you'll regret."

"I didn't want it to be this way. I didn't mean for it to happen." Bits of broken bottles littered his hair and a bead of sweat dripped down the side of his face. He wiped his cheek against his shoulder. "If you hadn't been here—"

"What? You wouldn't have broken into my place? You wouldn't have stolen from me?"

"You don't understand."

Out of the corner of her eye she saw Dean easing up his pant leg. "So tell me," she said, edging to the right, away from Dean. "Explain why you'd rather have drugs than a job and friends who trusted you. How you could betray the people who believed in you."

"I didn't want to hurt you. I never wanted you to find out." His eyes welled with tears and he rubbed at them with his free hand. "I just need some money, but this will be the only time. I swear. Then I'll get clean again."

For a moment she felt sorry for him. Then she remembered he was holding a gun on her. Had hurt Dean.

Meant to rob her. And she still wanted to help him? She was either pathetic or delusional.

"This isn't you, Richie. It's the drugs."

She licked her dry lips, noticed Dean slowly rising from his chair. Though he'd barely been able to walk, the gun in his hand was steady as a rock.

It was enough to chill her blood, and she shivered. Where did he get a gun? And more importantly, how was she going to stop either of them from using their weapons? How was she going to get them all out of this alive?

"You can still walk away," she said desperately to Richie. "No one's going to hurt you."

Tears streamed down his face and he lowered his arm. But he must've sensed Dean moving behind him, because he suddenly swung his gun around.

"No!" Adrenaline pulsing through her, Allie rushed at Richie, knocking her shoulder into him. The gun went off, the discharge sounding as loud as a cannon in the confined space. Through the ringing in her ears she thought she heard Dean shout. Richie shoved her and she landed hard against the counter of the sink, the breath momentarily knocked out of her. Before she could regain her footing, Richie backhanded her. Her head snapped to the side, fire exploding in her cheek.

Roaring like a cornered animal, Dean jumped onto a stool, then the bar, and with a flying leap, tackled Richie. Richie grunted at the force, his gun skidding across the floor. Allie scrambled through the puddles of alcohol and broken bottles, ignoring the stinging cuts to her palms and knees, her only thought on getting the gun. Helping Dean.

She picked it up, but could only hold it loosely

because of the bleeding gashes on her hands, the glass still embedded in her skin. *Just don't drop it,* she chanted silently to herself as she sat back on her butt and aimed the weapon at Richie.

Not that Dean needed her help, since he'd effectively knocked Richie out. She lowered her trembling arms and carefully set the weapon aside. Dean pulled his cell phone out as he straightened from Richie's prone body.

He knelt next to her as he called 911. After a quick, terse explanation of what had happened, he clicked the phone off and gently gripped her chin. His expression turned fierce as he studied her cheek, where Richie had hit her. But that was nothing compared to the fury in Dean's eyes when he noticed the blood on her hands.

He swore roundly, then shifted as if to stand.

"Don't," she said, skimming her fingertips over the back of his hand. Even with that light touch, she could feel the tension vibrating through him.

"Don't what?"

She nodded toward Richie. "He's already unconscious. There's no need to pound him some more."

"He hurt you. That's reason enough for me."

"Please. Just…could you just sit with me?"

He glanced at Richie, then at her before nodding. "Yeah, but let's get you out of this mess." He helped her to her feet and smoothed her hair back from her face. "You sure you're okay?"

His tenderness and concern mixed with her own relief that they were all alive, making her head swim. "I'm fine." She began to shiver in earnest. "Just more shaken than I'd like to admit. I'm also confused."

He guided her around the bar to the first stool. "You should know better than anyone there's no figuring out why people commit the crimes they do."

"No…I mean…yes, of course I'm curious why Richie would do this. But what I'm really wondering," she said as she searched Dean's face, "is what you're doing carrying a gun?"

DEAN INSERTED HIS KEY CARD into the lock and opened the motel door. He reached along the wall and flipped on the light. Used to working out of motel rooms, he never went anywhere without first locking all his files in a metal briefcase and making sure his laptop was shut off.

Which was a good thing, considering the way Allie was hovering over him.

"Want to lean on me?" she asked, as if a little bump on the head was enough to keep him down.

He gave her a look. "No."

She followed him inside, shut the door behind her. He didn't want her here. Not when he was feeling so amped up. So on edge.

So out of control.

"What is your problem?" she asked. "First you refuse to go to the hospital—"

"Me? You're the one who should've gone to the hospital instead of insisting the EMT take care of your cuts in the back of the ambulance."

She raised her bandaged palms. "Honestly, it looked much worse than it was." And after they'd taken the glass out of her knees and cleaned the cuts, Jack had given her a pair of Serenity Springs P.D. sweatpants to wear instead of her ruined jeans. "At least *I'm* not in danger of slipping into a coma."

"The EMT said I didn't even need stitches, so I doubt I'm heading into a vegetative state. Besides, what good would it have done to go to the E.R.?" He took his coat off, threw it onto the bed. "All they'd do is tell me I might have a mild concussion and to take it easy."

Even though his head had hurt like a son of a bitch, the four painkillers he'd downed earlier had diminished the agony to a dull ache.

He clenched his fists. He wished the pills would also do something to erase the memory of Allie throwing herself at that maniac. Of that bastard putting his hands on her.

"And now that you've seen me safely to my room," he continued as he sat on the bed and pulled one boot off, "you can go. A shower and a few hours of sleep and I'll be fine."

"Oh, yeah. That's a great idea. And what if you get dizzy in the shower? You could slip and crack your head open. Or be knocked unconscious again."

"I told you," he growled, "I was only out for a few minutes." He threw his second boot across the room and stood. "And I don't need a goddamn babysitter."

She tossed her purse onto the desk. "What has gotten into you?"

"You want to know? How about how, when your brother took our statements, you spun the facts so that while you didn't actually lie, you didn't tell the full story, either. If that's a sample of your skills, you must've been a hell of a lawyer."

"I didn't lie," she said, stepping up to him. "I told Jack what he needed to know. And how about you? You're the one carrying a concealed weapon."

"I have a permit."

"I don't like the idea of one of my employees being armed without my knowledge."

He edged closer until they were nose to nose. "That's the point of it being concealed."

And he could kick his own ass for switching from his preferred—and easily accessible—back holster to an ankle holster. All because she'd almost discovered his weapon that morning in her kitchen when they'd kissed.

"I don't like secrets," she maintained, crossing her arms.

"Oh, really? Then why don't we call Jack? Tell him some of the facts you left out before. Like how you threw yourself at a gun-waving drug addict!"

She tossed up her hands. "What was I supposed to do? Let him shoot you?"

"If that's what it took to keep you safe, then yes." He wrapped his fingers around her upper arms but resisted the urge to shake some sense into her. "Or did you think it'd be better if you got shot instead?"

She trembled, but since her expression was defiant and angry, he figured it wasn't because she was afraid of him. More than likely the adrenaline rush she'd been riding for the past two hours was waning.

Good. Reality would set in soon.

"I didn't want anyone to get shot. That was the point."

"Next time," he growled, lifting her onto her toes, "do me a favor and don't try to save me."

"Fine!"

"Great!"

Then he crushed her to him and kissed her. After a startled moment that felt more like a lifetime, she threw her arms around him.

Their tongues dueled as his hands raced over her. He couldn't stop touching her, assuring himself she really was safe. Whole.

His head ached but he didn't care. All he cared about was the woman in his arms. He speared his hands into her hair, held her head still while he kissed her deeply. She clawed at his shirt, lifted the hem and drew it over his head.

Pain rocked him and he grunted just loud enough for Allie to hear.

"Oh my God, I'm so sorry," she said. "Maybe we shouldn't—"

He kissed her again. No way was he allowing her to finish that sentence.

He spun them around and walked her backward until the backs of her legs hit the bed. She fell onto the mattress and he followed her down, pressing his hips against hers. He stopped kissing her only long enough to slip her shirt off.

They rolled so that she straddled him, and he reached behind her, unhooked her bra and slid it down her arms. He took one nipple in his mouth and sucked hard. She groaned and arched her back, curling her fingers into his chest.

They flipped again and he tugged her sweatpants down. She lifted her hips to help him, but the fabric bunched, caught on her boots. With a curse, he stood and, grasping them by the heels, pulled them off. She shimmied out of her pants and panties while he took his wallet out of his pocket and kicked the rest of his clothes off.

She scrambled to her knees on the bed, caressing his chest, trailing her unbandaged fingertips across his ribs and down his stomach. She skimmed her warm fingers over him and his hips bucked. She pressed against him, trapping his length between their bodies. He couldn't stop himself from sliding up the silky soft skin of her belly and down again. She scraped a fingernail over the tip of his erection and he bent his head for another voracious kiss even as he dug into his wallet. When he felt the square foil packet, he pinched it between his fingers and tossed the wallet aside.

He ripped open the package and sheathed himself before pushing her back onto the bed and settling between her legs. He pressed his erection between her curls and rubbed against her once. Twice.

"Dean," she gasped, raising her hips, "now. Please."

He gripped her hips and shifted so that he was at her entrance. Her heat, her wetness beckoned him but he held on to sanity, to what was left of his personal morals, long enough to keep from madly plunging into her.

"Allie," he said, sweat beading on his forehead, his arms shaking with the effort to hold himself back, "look at me." Her eyes opened, dark blue and filled with passion. "What's going on between us, what I feel for you, is real. Promise me you'll remember that."

"Dean, what—"

"Promise. Please."

She touched his face. "I promise," she whispered.

He kissed her and slid inside. And it was even better

than he'd imagined. He wanted to slow them down, wanted to make it last, but her eyes were at half-mast, her mouth open slightly. A soft flush stained her cheeks and she made a sound of contentment when he filled her.

She was driving him crazy.

When she wrapped her legs around his waist, crossing her feet at the ankles, his control snapped. He pumped into her like a madman. But she met him thrust for thrust. And when her breathing turned to soft gasps, he reached between them and stroked her. She tightened around him, her thighs gripping him, her back arched as her orgasm shook her body. Still he didn't stop. Couldn't. Their skin grew slick with sweat.

She leaned up and kissed him, bit his lower lip, then pushed against him until he rolled over. With her knees on either side of his thighs, she tucked her hips under, taking him deep inside. He gritted his teeth against the need to take control back from her. She bent forward, her peaked nipples dragging against his chest. She kissed him, his neck, his collarbones, his cheeks, her hair cascading around them, cool against his heated skin. Finally, she pressed her mouth against his in a languid kiss, her tongue sliding between his lips to lazily explore his mouth.

He groaned and shoved his hand into her hair.

She straightened and laid her bandaged hands flat on his chest, right above his racing heart. He'd been fighting his feelings for her, but when she smiled at him, he knew he couldn't hold out any longer.

Then she moved.

She undulated against him slowly, so slowly he gripped

the bedspread to keep from driving up into her. Her breasts swayed with her movements and he raised his head, catching one pink peak in his mouth. She made a mewling sound in the back of her throat and quickened her pace.

Needing to watch her, he let his head fall back, but replaced his mouth on her breast with his hands. He pinched her nipples and her mouth fell open, her hips working him like a piston.

It was torture. And heaven.

He held on to his control by a thin thread until her breathing accelerated and her nails dug into his chest.

Knowing she was close, he gripped her hips and rocked into her again and again until her body bowed back. She trembled as her second release engulfed her, and only then did he give himself over to the power of his own orgasm, calling her name as he emptied himself inside her.

CHAPTER FOURTEEN

ALLIE KEPT HER HEAD against Dean's chest, listening to the steady sound of his heart. She couldn't believe she wasn't a twitchy, hysterical mess after what had happened between them.

She sighed and snuggled further under the heavy comforter. Dean, having pulled her into his arms and tucked her head under his chin, had fallen asleep a few minutes ago. But his hold on her remained tight. Even in sleep, he couldn't stop touching her.

She wished she could shut her brain down long enough to doze off as well. But that wasn't happening. Not when she was worried about his head injury. She figured she'd wake him every thirty minutes or so to assure herself he hadn't slipped into a coma or something.

Good thing she had so many thoughts flying through her mind. They'd keep her awake.

She'd just had incredible sex with an amazing man.

An amazing man who worked for her. One who held a grudge against his brother—his entire family, really. Who had a hard time seeing more than his own point of view. Someone who kept secrets, such as the fact that he carried a gun.

She should be more nervous. More concerned about her possible lack of judgment. Should be contemplating how to sneak out of his room. Wondering how she'd be able to face him at work each day.

Instead, she wondered if, when she woke him to make sure he was okay, he'd want to have sex again.

She'd never felt better.

Her stomach growled. Well, except that she hadn't had anything to eat in over twelve hours. When her stomach rumbled again, she remembered the valentine's gift Dean had given her.

She carefully lifted his arm off her and slid out from beneath the covers. Gooseflesh rose on her bare skin and she put on Dean's discarded shirt and her socks. Not wanting to wake him, she picked up her purse and crept toward the bathroom.

A faint buzzing stopped her in her tracks. She frowned and looked down, realizing the sound came from Dean's jeans.

He mumbled something in his sleep and rolled over, the covers slipping down to reveal the strong planes of his back. She shook her head to get her focus off his body.

After a quick search of his pockets she found his phone and took it with her into the bathroom, shutting the door quietly. The name displayed on the screen was Nolan Winchester, along with an out-of-area number. After a few more buzzes, which she tried to muffle by putting a towel over the phone, the noise stopped.

She searched in her purse for the trail mix, opened it and, sitting on the edge of the tub, picked out the chocolate pieces first. Popping them into her mouth, she sighed in pleasure as they melted on her tongue.

Maybe she'd leave Dean a note and run out to get them some lunch. He was bound to be hungry when he woke up. She thought of the ugly bruise on his head. The swelling had gone down, but the skin had already turned an interesting shade of purple, and if she had to hazard a guess, she'd bet it hurt like hell.

She'd pick up some more painkillers, too. God knew they both could use them.

She ate some cranberries, then a few nuts. And because she'd been held at gunpoint not five hours ago and her hands were starting to sting again, she picked more chocolate pieces out of the bag.

When she was done she brushed her fingertips together and dug her own phone out of her purse to scroll through her missed calls. Two from Kelsey. Five from her mother. One from Jack.

Jack obviously hadn't wasted any time letting her family know what had happened.

She glanced at Dean's phone. Speaking of mothers and families wanting to know things… She picked up his cell. Nibbled her lower lip.

On the one hand, it was wrong of her to snoop through his recently received calls. Breach of privacy.

But on the other hand, it wasn't like she was reading his e-mails or snooping in his underwear drawer. All she wanted was his mother's phone number. The one she'd called him from last night.

Of course, it wasn't Allie's business—or her right— to call his mother about what had happened.

But Dean was hurt. If the situation was reversed and she'd been the one who'd been injured, she'd want someone to let her family know she was all right. And maybe Dean's mother would even have an idea about mending the rift between him and his family once and for all.

Allie flipped the phone open and scrolled through the recent calls until she reached the number listed under Home. Then, with a quick prayer that she had the right number—and was doing the right thing—she pressed the phone button.

The line rang twice before a woman answered, "Hello?"

"Hello, Mrs. Garret," she said, keeping her voice down, "this is Allison Martin from Serenity Springs, New York. I—"

"I'm so sorry, sugar, but I don't accept calls from telemarketers."

"Oh, no. I mean, I'm not a telemarketer. I'm a… friend of your son Dean. We work together at—"

"I had no idea Dean and Nolan had hired someone," she said. "What did you say your name was again, dear?"

Allie frowned. "Uh, Allie…Allison Martin." What was Dean's mother talking about? Him and Nolan hiring someone? "I'm sorry to bother you this early, and I don't want to alarm you, but I thought you'd want to know Dean was injured last night—"

"Is he all right?"

"He's fine. Just a mild concussion."

"I swear," Mrs. Garret said, her sweet Southern accent now steely, "I could skin that boy for putting himself in danger all the time. I thought when he came home from the marines he'd settle on an occupation that didn't turn my hair gray from worrying about him."

A chill climbed Allie's spine. "I'm sorry, Mrs. Garret, but I don't understand. What occupation are you talking about?" *Please be talking about Dean choosing to become a bartender. Please consider tending bar a dangerous occupation.*

"Why, Leatherneck Investigations, of course. Didn't you say you worked with him?"

Even through the roaring in her ears, Allie didn't miss the suspicion in the other woman's tone. "I…I don't work for Nolan and Dean's firm," she managed to say as she blinked back tears. "I'm working with Dean on a, uh, case he's investigating. It's a…a one-time thing." She cleared her throat. "Mrs. Garret, I'm so sorry to cut you off, but I have to go."

"That's fine. Thank you so much for letting me know. And will you please have Dean call me? I'll feel better when I hear from him."

Allie's fingers grew slippery on the phone. She switched ears and wiped her bandaged palm down the front of her—of Dean's—shirt. "Of course," she croaked. "Goodbye."

She didn't wait for a response, just ended the call. Pain welled in her chest, made it impossible for her to breathe. She wrapped her arms around herself and rocked back and forth. Concentrated on inhaling. Then exhaling. Slowly. Steadily.

Dean's mother was wrong. She had to be.

There was one way to know for sure.

Allie picked up her own cell phone and dialed a familiar number. Waited for an answer.

"It's me," she said. "We might have a problem."

"YOU BASTARD."

Dean shot awake and sat up, only to fall back onto the pillow with a grunt of pain as one hundred fifteen pounds of pissed-off female landed on him.

"Allie, what—" He broke off when she went after him with her fists and forearms. He raised both arms but she continued to pummel him. "What's the matter with you?"

"I can't believe how naive I was." She landed a vicious punch above his ear, and that's when he noticed she'd unwrapped the gauze from around her hands. "How stupid." Another blow, this time on his chin, made his teeth snap together.

Jack Martin must've given her self-defense lessons because she had a wicked right hook. She came at Dean with everything she had: fists, forearms, elbows, feet and knees. His jaw throbbed, matching the ache in his temple.

"Ow," he growled when she threw an elbow at his already sore head. "Okay, that's enough. You're going to hurt your hands."

"It won't be enough until you're broken and bleeding," she promised.

Damn but she was bloodthirsty. And considering it was his blood she wanted to shed, he put a stop to it.

He sat up again, throwing her off balance long enough to flip her onto her back. He held both her wrists in one hand and captured her arms above her head.

"Get off," she demanded, bucking wildly beneath him. "I'm not done kicking your ass!"

"The hell you're not," he grunted. She brought her knee up and he rolled in time to avoid being unmanned. He hated when people fought dirty. "Knock it off." He wrapped his legs around hers and pinned them down. "I don't want to hurt you—"

She sobbed softly. "You don't want to hurt me? *I* want to do some major damage to *you*."

But her words lacked the heat she'd come at him with earlier. Worse, tears had begun to leak out, down into her hairline. He met her eyes, caught his breath at the depth of pain he saw there.

His stomach dropped. She knew. He had no idea how she'd found out and it didn't matter. There was no way he'd be able to make her understand. To get her to forgive him.

But he couldn't go down without a fight. "Allie, I—"

"You're nothing but a liar," she said, making it sound far worse than any other name he'd been called. "And I was stupid enough to believe you." She turned her head and shut her eyes. "Now get off me."

He let go of her wrists and rolled to the side. Laid there staring blindly at the ceiling as she sprang from the bed. *Shit.* He never should have touched her when there were so many lies between them.

Resigned, he stood and put his jeans on. "How did you find out?" he asked quietly

"That you're not a bartender?" She yanked her sweatpants up over her hips. "That you're a partner in Leatherneck Investigations, a private investigation firm specializing in missing persons cases?" She snatched the shirt she'd worn last night off the floor. "Your mother told me."

"You talked to my mother?"

"Don't worry, she didn't mean to blow your cover." Allie sat on the chair and pulled her boots on. "Actually, I probably still wouldn't know if I hadn't called to tell her you'd been hurt. I thought maybe the two of us could figure out a way to reconcile you and your brother." She got to her feet, her hands clenched at her sides. "Jack's always saying someday my nose is going to get bent out of joint if I keep putting it where it doesn't belong. He was right."

She picked up her jacket and purse and stalked toward the door. Dean got there first, though, standing in front of it, his legs spread, his arms crossed. "You're not leaving until we've talked this through."

"Do you really want to add unlawful imprisonment to your growing list of crimes?"

He felt as if he was losing something vital. Something he'd never be able to get back. And he couldn't prevent it.

"Don't you even want to know why I lied?" he asked almost desperately. "Or who I'm investigating?"

She pulled her cell phone out of her purse. "If you don't move by the time I count to three, I'm calling Jack. One…"

"You don't need to ask because you already know."

"Two…"

Why did she have to be so stubborn? "I don't want to hurt her—I didn't mean to hurt anyone. I want to help—"

"Three." Allie flipped open the phone.

Fine. He'd already lost her; he'd be damned if he'd lose this case as well. He leaned back against the door. "You don't want to do that."

"Oh, yes, I do."

"When Jack gets here to arrest me, I'm sure he'll be very interested in hearing how you helped Lynne Addison escape her husband."

Allie's hand shook as she closed her phone. But she didn't put it away. "I—I don't know what you're talking about."

"Lynne Addison doesn't have custody of her son, and she's wanted for his kidnapping." Dean studied her face, saw the panic. And felt like a total ass for putting it there. But he had to get her to listen. "And you could be charged with assisting in a child abduction."

She sneered. "You're not very good at your job, are you? I told you before, I haven't seen Lynne Addison in almost two years."

He narrowed his eyes. "Now who's lying?"

"You don't have any evidence I helped Lynne. Which means it's your word against mine. And which one of us do you think Jack is going to believe?"

Dean nodded. "He'll believe you, of course. But who said I didn't have proof?"

HE WAS BLUFFING. He had to be.

But she could see in his eyes that he wasn't.

Her head reeled. What had she done wrong?

She'd trusted him. She should've listened to Jack and Kelsey and never let Dean into her life. Or into her heart.

She slowly lowered the phone. "If you're looking for Lynne, why didn't you just ask me if I knew where she was? Why all the lies?"

"I couldn't take the chance of you tipping her off. I figured she'd get spooked and run again." Dean looked at Allie beseechingly. "All you have to do is tell me where they are. I promise, I'm not out to hurt them."

Her knees almost buckled. He didn't know. Not everything. Not the most important thing—where Lynne and Jon were. *Who* they were.

"It wouldn't have mattered if you'd asked or not," she said, "because I don't know where they are. I didn't help them—"

"You did it to appease your guilt for helping Miles get acquitted." Dean gestured to her phone. "You called several different numbers over the past few months, all to prepaid cell phones—"

"How do you know…?" She felt as if he'd punched her in the stomach. "I didn't lose my phone last week. You took it."

He had the good grace to avert his gaze. "The last prepaid number had a Cincinnati area code. Which is where a woman and child matching Lynne and Jon's descriptions were spotted at a hospital emergency room."

Allie shook her head. "You're wrong."

"Am I? So you didn't plan for Lynne to stop at that bookstore where one of your ex-clients worked? An ex-client who'd be more than happy to pay you back by helping another woman get away from an abusive husband?" Something on her face must've given her away because Dean's expression softened. "I know about Sarah Lambert. Tell me, how did you do it? Did Sarah sneak the two out the back? Hide them at the store until it was safe for you to smuggle them out of town?"

She began to shake. From anger, she told herself, not because he was so close to the truth.

She was afraid of what was going to happen next. She might not be able to protect Lynne and Jon anymore.

"I—I have to go." She stepped toward the door, but he didn't move away.

"Haven't you done enough? You've carried this responsibility for so long, Allie. You've given her your savings, even gave up your career. You've paid your penance. Tell me where they are." He reached for her. "Let me help you."

She stepped back. "You want to help me? After everything you've done, the way you manipulated me and my feelings, I'm supposed to trust what you say?" She shoved both hands into her hair. "You must think I'm a complete idiot. Well, why wouldn't you? The way I ate up every word you said."

"It wasn't like that—"

"You must be so proud of yourself. And hey, you really went above and beyond. But you didn't have to sleep with me. I'd already bought your act."

"What happened between us last night was real. If we could sit down, talk this through—"

"I don't want to talk to you. I don't want to *look* at you."

"Damn it, Allie, I care about you."

She slapped him. Hard. "Don't," she said shakily, her cut palm stinging. Tears clogged her throat. "Just… don't. Please…let me go."

She didn't know if her slap made him finally move away from the door, or the pathetic plea in her voice. She didn't care. She had to get away from him and figure out a way to fix this before it was too late for Lynne and Jon.

She opened the door and stepped out into the bright sunshine. The cold air.

"I can help you," Dean said from the doorway. "And Lynne."

Allie faced him. "You expect me to believe that? How, by forcing her back to her husband?"

"I'm not working for her husband. I'm working for her mother. And she wants to see her daughter and grandson. She wants to help them."

Allie clasped her hands together to stop herself from slapping him again. "And that's the last lie you'll ever tell me. Lynne's mother couldn't have hired you," she managed to retort hoarsely. "She's been dead for over a year."

CHAPTER FIFTEEN

DEAN POUNDED ON THE DOOR of the small house. He couldn't believe he'd been so blind he hadn't seen what was in front of his face this whole time.

He banged again and then stepped over to the large window, cupped his hands around his eyes and peered into a tidy living room. No lights. And the driveway was empty except for the tire tracks in the snow.

Was he too late?

He hunched his shoulders and surveyed the neighborhood. It was early afternoon, and the street was quiet. The only sign of life was the smoke rising in a plume from the chimney next door. He'd turned to head back down the steps when a familiar vehicle parked three houses down caught his eye.

He spun back around and hit his open hand against the door. "Allie?" he called. "I saw your car. If you're in there, let me in."

He held his breath as he waited. Finally, he heard the clicking sound of a dead bolt being unlocked, and the door opened.

Allie stood in the doorway in an oversize sweater, jeans, and the boots she'd had on when she'd left his motel room a few hours ago. She hugged her arms around herself. "Guess you're better at your job than I thought."

He didn't reply. Couldn't. Her hair was pulled back into a messy ponytail and her eyes were red-rimmed as if she'd been crying.

She looked…broken. Because of what he'd done.

"Can I come in?" he asked.

She shrugged. "Why not? It doesn't matter what you do now."

He stepped inside and shut the door while she perched on the edge of the worn couch. The room was sparsely furnished—with just a sofa, an armchair, a wooden bench used for a coffee table and an upturned crate by the sofa with a lamp. A small TV sat on an old dresser against the wall by the staircase. There were no pictures on the walls, no framed photos to show who lived here.

Dean pulled the rolled up folder out of his back pocket and tapped it against his hand. He wanted to sit next to Allie and take her in his arms, to assure her that everything would be okay. But she wouldn't believe him, so what was the point?

She picked up a red Lego piece from the floor. Turned it end over end. "How'd you figure it out?"

"That Ellen Jensen and her son, Bobby, are really Lynne and Jon Addison?"

She nodded once and tossed the Lego onto the table.

"After you left, I asked Nolan, my partner, to figure out who was masquerading as Robin Hawley and why she hired us."

Allie frowned. "You really didn't know she wasn't Lynne's mother?"

He clenched his hands, bending the file. He couldn't believe he and Nolan had been tricked. Or that Allie thought he'd knowingly work for a scumbag like Miles Addison.

"I swear, neither one of us knew." She averted her eyes and he couldn't tell whether she believed him or not. "While Nolan checked out Robin Hawley's story, I thought I'd better double-check everything she'd told us, all the information she'd given us." He pulled out a photo and tossed it on the table beside the Lego piece. "That's when I came across this."

She picked up the color picture of Lynne taken five years ago. Glanced at it and then set it down again. "Lynne Addison doesn't exist anymore."

"No. I guess she doesn't. I knew Ellen looked familiar, but I couldn't place her." Because the last he knew, Lynne was a curvy, fashionable, green-eyed blonde. Not a frumpy brown-eyed brunette. "The eyes threw me the most. Colored contacts?" he asked.

"So now you know," Allie said, ignoring his question. "What are you going to do?"

He set the file on the table. "Nolan found out that Robin Hawley is actually Sondra Wilkins."

Her mouth popped open. "Miles's secretary?"

Dean gritted his teeth. The idea of him and Nolan being so easily tricked still pissed him off. "Seems her skills are more diverse than just running Addison's office. She's also one hell of an actress. She played the part of repentant mother to a T."

"Next time you should check out your client's background," Allie said bitterly.

Unable to stop himself, he asked, "Like you did before you hired me?"

He was surprised she didn't shove the Lego down his throat. "I hope you don't have to give back any retainer she paid you. I'd hate for you to be out any money."

Right. More like she hoped he'd drop dead where he stood so she could spit on his cold, lifeless body. "Actually, we told her we were still on the case. In a few days we'll tell her our leads ended somewhere west of the Mississippi. We were thinking Montana or Wyoming."

Her eyes narrowed. "Why would you do that?"

"So when Addison hires someone else to find her— and I'm guessing he will—it'll throw them off the real trail." He shoved his hands in his pockets. "Nolan and I have a strict need-to-know policy with our clients. Ever since one of our first customers showed up in the same town where we'd tracked his teenage runaway daughter. Once she saw him, our cover was blown and we learned a valuable lesson. So Lynne—or Ellen— doesn't have to worry about Miles knowing she's here in Serenity Springs."

"Doesn't matter. Because she's not here."

"I know you're mad at me, but you need to stop the act." He jabbed a finger at the picture. "*Ellen* needs to be prepared when the next PI comes looking for her, and I need her to know—" He clamped his mouth shut.

Allie laughed harshly. "You need her to know what? That you're sorry? That you didn't mean to ruin her life?"

"Yes, damn it," he growled. "I am sorry. I didn't mean for any of this to happen."

"Well, you can forget about me passing on your

apology. She's gone. And before you ask, I don't know where she went and I doubt she'll be in contact with me anytime soon." Allie picked up a folded piece of paper from the table and threw it at him. It fluttered to the floor at his feet. "Looks like you won't be absolved of this particular sin."

He picked up the paper, unfolded it and read the neat writing: *"Allie, thank you for everything but it's time we were on our own."*

He crumpled it in his hand. "Is this for real?"

"The closets are empty. She must've taken off right after I called her this morning." Allie slowly got to her feet as if it hurt to move. "It's over."

He stood frozen to the spot as she walked to the door without a backward glance. He followed, brushing past her and jumping off the porch onto the sidewalk, blocking her.

"It doesn't have to be over," he said. *"We* don't have to be over."

She shook her head. "You're kidding, right? After everything you've done, all your lies, you think there's anything left between us?"

He'd been in worse situations than this, he reminded himself. He'd been shot at, had things blown up next to him. He'd lost his son.

He wouldn't lose Allie. He couldn't.

He swallowed and reached for her hand, but the glare she shot him told him he needed to keep his distance. "Please, Allie."

She inclined her head and he breathed a sigh of relief.

"I'm not proud of any of this," he said. "Not how I allowed myself to be used by that prick to find his wife.

And I'm not proud that I lied to you. I actually…I was going to tell you last night—"

"That's convenient."

"It's the truth. When I went outside to warm up the cars I knew I needed to come clean with you. I realized I…cared about you and I didn't want any lies between us anymore." He prayed she believed him. One last time. "But then Richie knocked me out and—"

"And you decided you no longer needed to tell me?" She glanced around and lowered her voice, even though they were alone. "You thought you'd sleep with me instead?"

"I didn't mean for that to happen."

"I trusted you," she declared, shivering in the cold. "I told you things I'd never told anyone." Tears slid unchecked down her cheeks. "You used me. And for what? A job?"

"I was wrong," he said, hating the desperation he heard in his voice. "But I can make it up to you. I know I can."

"You can't," she whispered. "It's too late."

His anger simmered. "So that's it? You just—" he snapped his fingers "—and we're through?"

"You're the one who lied—"

"You're willing to forgive Richie for holding a gun to your head, but not me."

"That's right, I can forgive Richie. He didn't betray me like you did."

Dean's jaw dropped. "Didn't betray you?" he asked incredulously. "He showed up for work high. He lied to you. He stole from you—"

"He didn't break my heart," she cried. "But you did."

Dean couldn't catch his breath. "Allie, I—"

She ran past him, down the street.

And he didn't know how he'd ever get her back.

MONDAY EVENING not even the latest song by Beyoncé, currently blasting out of her portable CD player, could lighten Allie's mood. Not when she'd spent a sleepless night worrying about Lynne and Jon.

And thinking about Dean.

She wiped the back of her hand against her forehead and gripped the edge of the ugly wallpaper, tearing a long sheet off the wall. She was angry—at him for betraying her, at herself for believing him—not because he'd hurt her. For him to hurt her would mean she cared more for Dean than she was willing to admit. It would mean that the tears she'd cried last night were because she'd lost her chance at something special.

The cuts on her palms weren't yet completely healed but she needed to do something to keep busy. It was tear apart either her kitchen or The Summit, and at least she could be alone in her kitchen.

She crumpled the wallpaper and threw it across the room. Persephone gave chase.

"You throw like a girl."

She jumped, glaring at Dillon before shutting the music off. "I'm not in the mood."

"From the looks of it," he said, taking in the torn wallpaper still on the walls and the balls of it littering the floor, "you're in a scary mood."

"Don't you even knock?" she asked, spraying solution on the wall to loosen the glue.

"I knocked," he assured her. "But when you didn't answer, I thought I'd better let myself in."

She really needed to start remembering to keep her door locked at all times. "I'm sort of in the middle of something..." She wiped her sticky hands on her threadbare jeans. "So unless this is important, can it wait until tomorrow?"

Dillon kicked a pile of scraps out of his way as he crossed to the table. "No. Kelsey asked me to check up on you." He sat down. "She's worried."

Allie's lower lip trembled so she bit it. "I told her when I called that I'm not feeling well. That's all."

"Funny, Kelsey said she tried to get your new bartender to work tonight, but he wasn't answering his phone. Is he sick, too?"

A lump formed in her throat. "I—I don't want to talk about it," she stuttered, keeping her back to Dillon.

"Okay."

She turned and eyed him suspiciously. "That's it?"

"Sure. Hey, you got anything to drink?"

"In the fridge." He got up and opened the door, took out two bottles of beer. "Help yourself," she told him drily.

He grinned. "I got one for you, too."

"I don't want one," she said, not caring if she sounded petulant. She wanted to be left alone.

"Then sit with me while I have mine." He hooked his foot around the leg of a chair and pulled it out. "Come on. You can finish destroying your kitchen as soon as I'm done."

She huffed out an exasperated breath and dropped into the chair. "Fine."

Dillon retook his seat and opened both beers. Slid one toward her. She rolled her eyes and pushed up the sleeves of her baggy sweatshirt before reaching for it and taking a drink.

He raised his bottle as if making a toast. "Nina said yes."

Allie froze, the beer halfway back to her lips. She squeezed his hand. "Congratulations. I'm so happy for you."

He touched his bottle to hers. "Thank you. Now, quit messing with me and tell me what's wrong."

She sat back, placing both hands in her lap. "You said I didn't have to talk about it."

"I lied."

She was too raw. "I can't."

"I'm warning you, if I don't get the story, Kelsey's going to send Jack over here next. The only reason he didn't come tonight is because he's working."

Allie tipped her head back. And wouldn't that be the perfect ending? To have her brother know all about her latest—and greatest—screwup. "I don't want Jack, I don't want *anyone* to know. Not Kelsey. Not Nina. No one."

He nodded slowly. "You have my word."

"I ruined everything," she whispered.

She filled him in on the whole story—from her representing Miles, to helping Lynne and Jon escape, to finding out about Dean's investigation. She managed to get through her confession dry eyed, but when she finished, she felt as drained as if she'd just run a marathon.

Dillon whistled. "When you break the law, you go all out."

She sipped her beer. "I did it for a good cause. But now Lynne's on the run again and has no one to help her."

"You already gave her money and helped her get away from a bad situation."

"That's what Dean said," Allie admitted. "But it was my fault her husband wasn't in prison where he belonged. What else was I supposed to do?"

"Sounds like you did everything you could." He leaned back. Picked at the label on his bottle. "The cowboy did a number on you, huh?"

And the last thing she wanted was to think about how Dean had made a fool of her. Or worse, her conflicted feelings over him. "He lied to me."

Dillon waited patiently, as if he had all the time in the world. "He said he didn't want to scare Lynne off," she added. "That he wasn't sure what I knew."

"And if he'd asked, straight out, if you knew where Lynne was, what would you have done?"

"I don't see what that has to do with any—"

"What would you have done?"

She squirmed, realized she was, and forced herself to sit still. "I wouldn't have told him. But that's different."

"Doesn't seem so different to me. And all this time," her friend continued mildly, "when someone asked you why you quit your job and moved back to Serenity Springs, what did you do?"

Her stomach turned. "I never lied to you or my family."

But guilt pinched her. She hadn't been completely honest in so long, she was afraid she'd forgotten how.

"So omitting certain information is all right? As long as you're the one doing it?"

Stricken, she sat up. "That's not fair. I didn't want you all to know how I failed."

"So your pride kept you from telling us what really happened. From helping you during a difficult time?"

She drummed her fingers on the table. "You know, if Jack were here listening to me, at least he'd want to go kick Dean's ass."

"I'm not saying I don't. But if there's one thing I've learned the past few months it's that our fears can keep us from what we really want. They can keep us from living the life we're meant to live. They can even keep us from being with the people we're meant to be with." He paused as if letting that wisdom sink in.

But she didn't want it to sink in. She just wanted to stop hurting. And more importantly, to stop wanting Dean.

"Did the cowboy say why he didn't tell you what he was really doing here?" Dillon asked.

"Not that it matters," she said, holding on to her righteous anger as tightly as possible, "but he said he was trying to reconcile a woman with her family. That he didn't know the client who'd hired him worked for Miles."

"Reuniting a family sounds like something *you'd* do," Dillon stated.

Her face heated as she remembered she'd tried to do exactly that yesterday when she'd called Dean's mother.

But Allie hadn't lied to him. Well, she had, but it had been for the greater good. She had to keep Lynne and Jon safe.

Her actions were justified.

Weren't they?

Dillon finished his beer and stood. "I guess I'll be going, since you've got it all figured out."

"I do." So why did she feel so sick? So unsure? "It's for the best that Dean's gone. I can't trust him."

"This isn't about trust," Dillon said, his expression understanding and—to her horror—pitying. "It's about forgiveness. And the first person you need to forgive is yourself. Once you've done that, you'll be able to forgive him. And maybe, just maybe, you'll also be brave enough to give him a second chance. To give you both a second chance."

DEAN STEPPED INTO The Summit's kitchen. He'd waited until late afternoon, knowing the bar would be empty, then paid Noreen a hundred bucks to keep Kelsey occupied in the office long enough for Dean to slip into the building unnoticed. He took his hat off and stood in the doorway. Allie had her back to him as she worked at the counter. A sense of déjà vu hit him so hard, he had to grip the doorjamb to remain upright.

It'd been one month since he'd first seen Allie shaking her hips at the stove. And over two weeks since he'd seen her last.

The longest two weeks of his life.

"Hello, Allie."

She spun around, a knife in one hand, a large onion in the other. He drank in the sight of her. Her hair was braided and she had on jeans and a long-sleeved T-shirt. She'd never looked more beautiful.

Or stunned.

She finally blinked and shut her mouth. "Dean," she said, setting the knife and onion back on the counter and wiping her hands down the front of her jeans. "What are you doing here?"

Not quite an enthusiastic response, but she hadn't thrown anything at him or called the cops on him, so things were going better than he'd hoped.

"These are for you," he said as he crossed the room. He held out the bouquet of red lilies he'd picked up at the florist down the block. She made no move to take them so he thrust them at her, forcing her to accept them or let them fall to the floor. "And in case you're thinking about dropping them off at the hospital, I want you to know I already ordered a dozen bouquets of something called gerbera daisies to be delivered there. The lady at the floral shop said they were real cheerful flowers so the patients should like them."

"You sent flowers to the hospital?"

"Yes, ma'am, I did."

She shook her head as if coming out of a trance. "I thought you went back to Texas."

He switched his hat to his other hand. Prayed he wouldn't blow this, not when she was at least listening to him. "That's right. After you walked away from me, I took the first flight I could get. I figured the best thing to do was pretend none of this ever happened." He inhaled deeply but couldn't get rid of the constricted feeling in his chest. "It was easier than staying and risking you not forgiving me."

"And yet here you are," she said softly, but he couldn't tell if she was happy about that or not.

Please, God, let her be happy about it.

"I did a lot of thinking when I got home. Hell, all I did for a week was think about the choices I'd made. I was too scared to work at my marriage and I let my pride and anger keep me from my family for two years." He tossed his hat on the table before reaching for his wallet. He pulled a picture out of it. "I figured since I couldn't fix what happened between us, I should do everything in my power to fix the other aspects of my life. Starting with my family."

He handed her the picture, waited while she set the flowers down on a chair before taking it. Noticed that her hand wasn't quite steady.

He watched her face as she looked at the picture of him holding a little girl. "Is this…"

He nodded. "That's Rene Susan. My niece."

Allie's expression softened. "She's beautiful."

"She is. Which is surprising, since she takes after her daddy."

Allie handed him the picture back and smiled. "Sounds like you made some real progress with your family."

"It wasn't easy," he admitted, sliding the picture back into his wallet. "I thought for sure they wouldn't forgive me. That I didn't deserve forgiveness."

"Is that why you're here? Absolution?"

He swallowed. "I'm here to fight for you."

"What?"

"I can't stop thinking about you. I know it's going to take time to learn to trust me again, so I'm going to stick it out until that day comes." He did what he'd been wanting to do since he first walked into the room—he touched her. Just a light brush of his fingertip down her cheek, but when she didn't flinch, his heart soared. "I want to be with you, Allie," he said huskily. "I want you in my life. No matter what it takes."

She stepped back and his hope waned. "I haven't done much else but think about what happened. Between us. And with Lynne and Jon. You were right," she said, glancing at him, "I was so scared of not being able to make it up to them that I lost myself. And when I found out the reason you were here I realized I wouldn't be able to protect them any longer. Yet I felt I had to. To make up for what I'd done."

She still blamed herself. He hated that she couldn't see all the good she'd done. "You did all you could for them."

"It doesn't seem like enough. And when I think about them living their lives on the run… I really thought they could settle in Serenity Springs and be safe."

He was suffused with guilt for his part in it, anger for how he and Nolan had been fooled. "And they would've been safe if it wasn't for me."

"No. I wanted to blame you, but I know as long as Miles is searching for them, they'll never be safe." She tucked her hair behind her ear. "I…I appreciate you and your partner sending Miles on a wild-goose chase."

"I hope it worked."

She nodded. Licked her lips. "I've missed you," she blurted, blushing.

His heart raced. "Darlin', you don't know how happy I am to hear that."

He reached for her but she evaded him, crossing to the side table by the back door. She picked up her purse. "You're lucky you got here when you did," she said, rifling through her bag. She pulled out an envelope. "I'm taking a trip tomorrow, and since I wasn't sure how long I'd be gone, Kelsey is going to run the bar for me until I get back."

"Are you returning to New York?" Though he told himself that would be best for her, he couldn't help but wonder if she meant to start over. Without him.

"No. Not New York."

She handed him an airplane ticket. He frowned and then glanced at it. And did a double take when he read the destination.

He caught his breath. "Dallas?"

Her eyes shone with unshed tears. "I was coming after you."

He tipped his head back. "Thank God." Then he pulled her into his arms and kissed her. "I'll never lie to you again," he promised, moments later. "I love you, Allison Martin."

She smiled. "I love you, too, Dean Garret." She fiddled with the button on his shirt and glanced up at him from under her eyelashes. "As a matter of fact, why don't you and I sneak out of here? We can go back to my house, and I can show you just how much I love you…."

He pressed his lips to her forehead. "That's the best idea I've heard in weeks."

He kissed her again and when they drew apart, they

were both breathing hard. She was already reaching for her coat. "Oh, and don't forget your hat." The glint in her eyes was wicked. "Unless you have something against wearing it in bed?"

He laughed and settled his Stetson on his head. "No, ma'am, I surely don't."

* * * * *

*Celebrate 60 years of pure reading pleasure
with Harlequin®!*

To commemorate the event, Silhouette Special
Edition invites you to Ashley O'Ballivan's bed-
and-breakfast in the small town of Stone Creek.
The beautiful innkeeper will have her hands full
caring for her old flame Jack McCall. He's on the
run and recovering from a mysterious illness, but
that won't stop him from trying to win Ashley back.

*Enjoy an exclusive glimpse of Linda Lael Miller's
AT HOME IN STONE CREEK
Available in November 2009 from
Silhouette Special Edition®*

The helicopter swung abruptly sideways in a dizzying arch, setting Jack McCall's fever-ravaged brain spinning.

His friend's voice sounded tinny, coming through the earphones. "You belong in a hospital," he said. "Not some backwater bed-and-breakfast."

All Jack really knew about the virus raging through his system was that it wasn't contagious, and there was no known treatment for it besides a lot of rest and quiet. "I don't like hospitals," he responded, hoping he sounded like his normal self. "They're full of sick people."

Vince Griffin chuckled but it was a dry sound, rough at the edges. "What's in Stone Creek, Arizona?" he asked. "Besides a whole lot of nothin'?"

Ashley O'Ballivan was in Stone Creek, and she was a whole lot of somethin', but Jack had neither the strength nor the inclination to explain. After the way he'd ducked out six months before, he didn't expect a welcome, knew he didn't deserve one. But Ashley, being Ashley, would take him in whatever her misgivings.

He had to get to Ashley; he'd be all right.

He closed his eyes, letting the fever swallow him.

There was no telling how much time had passed

when he became aware of the chopper blades slowing overhead. Dimly, he saw the private ambulance waiting on the airfield outside of Stone Creek; it seemed that twilight had descended.

Jack sighed with relief. His clothes felt clammy against his flesh. His teeth began to chatter as two figures unloaded a gurney from the back of the ambulance and waited for the blades to stop.

"Great," Vince remarked, unsnapping his seat belt. "Those two look like volunteers, not real EMTs."

The chopper bounced sickeningly on its runners, and Vince, with a shake of his head, pushed open his door and jumped to the ground, head down.

Jack waited, wondering if he'd be able to stand on his own. After fumbling unsuccessfully with the buckle on his seat belt, he decided not.

When it was safe the EMTs approached, following Vince, who opened Jack's door.

His old friend Tanner Quinn stepped around Vince, his grin not quite reaching his eyes.

"You look like hell warmed over," he told Jack cheerfully.

"Since when are you an EMT?" Jack retorted.

Tanner reached in, wedged a shoulder under Jack's right arm and hauled him out of the chopper. His knees immediately buckled, and Vince stepped up, supporting him on the other side.

"In a place like Stone Creek," Tanner replied, "everybody helps out."

They reached the wheeled gurney, and Jack found himself on his back.

Tanner and the second man strapped him down, a process that brought back a few bad memories.

"Is there even a hospital in this place?" Vince asked irritably from somewhere in the night.

"There's a pretty good clinic over in Indian Rock," Tanner answered easily, "and it isn't far to Flagstaff." He paused to help his buddy hoist Jack and the gurney into the back of the ambulance. "You're in good hands, Jack. My wife is the best veterinarian in the state."

Jack laughed raggedly at that.

Vince muttered a curse.

Tanner climbed into the back beside him, perched on some kind of fold-down seat. The other man shut the doors.

"You in any pain?" Tanner said as his partner climbed into the driver's seat and started the engine.

"No." Jack looked up at his oldest and closest friend and wished he'd listened to Vince. Ever since he'd come down with the virus—a week after snatching a five-year-old girl back from her non-custodial parent, a small-time Colombian drug dealer—he hadn't been able to think about anyone or anything but Ashley. When he *could* think, anyway.

Now, in one of the first clearheaded moments he'd experienced since checking himself out of Bethesda the day before, he realized he might be making a major mistake. Not by facing Ashley—he owed her that much and a lot more. No, he could be putting her in danger, putting Tanner and his daughter and his pregnant wife in danger, too.

"I shouldn't have come here," he said, keeping his voice low.

Tanner shook his head, his jaw clamped down hard as though he was irritated by Jack's statement.

"This is where you belong," Tanner insisted. "If you'd had sense enough to know that six months ago, old buddy, when you bailed on Ashley without so much as a fare-thee-well, you wouldn't be in this mess."

Ashley. The name had run through his mind a million times in those six months, but hearing somebody say it out loud was like having a fist close around his insides and squeeze hard.

Jack couldn't speak.

Tanner didn't press for further conversation.

The ambulance bumped over country roads, finally hitting smooth blacktop.

"Here we are," Tanner said. "Ashley's place."

* * * * *

*Will Jack be able to
patch things up with Ashley, or will his
past put the woman he loves in harm's way?
Find out in
AT HOME IN STONE CREEK
by Linda Lael Miller
Available November 2009 from
Silhouette Special Edition®*

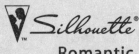

HARLEQUIN® *Romance.*

This November,
queen of the rugged rancher

PATRICIA THAYER

teams up with

DONNA ALWARD

to bring you an extra-special treat
this holiday season—

two romantic stories
in one book!

Join sisters Amelia and Kelley for Christmas at
Rocking H Ranch where these feisty cowgirls swap
presents for proposals, mistletoe for marriage and
experience the unbeatable rush of falling in love!

Available in November wherever books are sold.

www.eHarlequin.com

HR17619

REQUEST YOUR FREE BOOKS!

2 FREE NOVELS PLUS 2 FREE GIFTS!

HARLEQUIN®

Super Romance®

Exciting, emotional, unexpected!

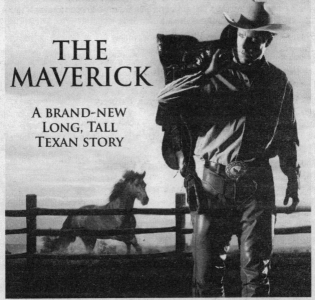

Silhouette® Desire

HARLEQUIN® Super Romance®

COMING NEXT MONTH

Available November 10, 2009

#1596 LIKE FATHER, LIKE SON • Karina Bliss
The Diamond Legacy
What's worse? Discovering his heritage is a lie or following in his grandfather's footsteps? All Joe Fraser *does* know is that Philippa Browne is pregnant and he's got to do right by her. Too bad she has her own ideas about motherhood…and marriage.

#1597 HER SECRET RIVAL • Abby Gaines
Those Merritt Girls
Taking over her father's law firm isn't just the professional opportunity of a lifetime— it's a chance for Megan Merritt to finally get close to him. Winning a lucrative divorce case is her way to prove she's the one for the job. Except the opposing lawyer in the divorce is Travis Jamieson, who is also after her dad's job!

#1598 A CONFLICT OF INTEREST • Anna Adams
Welcome to Honesty
Jake Sloane knows right from wrong—as a judge, it's his responsibility. Until he meets Maria Keaton, he's never blurred that line. Now his attraction to her is tearing him between what his head knows he should do and what his heart wants.

#1599 HOME FOR THE HOLIDAYS • Sarah Mayberry
Single Father
Raising his kids on his own is a huge learning curve for Joe Lawson. So does he really have time to fall for the unconventional woman next door, Hannah Napier? Time or not, that's what's happening.…

#1600 A MAN WORTH LOVING • Kimberly Van Meter
Home in Emmett's Mill
Aubrey Rose can't stand Sammy Halvorsen when they first meet. She agrees to be a nanny to his infant son only because she's a sucker for babies. As she gets to know Sammy, however, she starts to fall for him. But how to make him realize he's a man worth loving?

#1601 UNEXPECTED GIFTS • Holly Jacobs
9 Months Later
Elinore Cartright has her hands full overseeing the teen parenting program, especially when she discovers *she's* unexpectedly expecting. Not how she envisioned her forties, but life's unpredictable. So is her friend Zac Keller, who suddenly wants to date her *and* be a daddy, too!

HSRCNMBPA1009